OCTOBER

MARK FASSETT

OTHER BOOKS BY MARK FASSETT

The Sacrifice of Mendleson Moony
Minders

A Wizard's Work
Shattered
Fragments
* Bloodweave

Lords Of Genova
Questioner's Shadow

Grim Repo Files
Grim Repo
Parted Out

Novellas
Dreams of Earth
A Tower Without Doors
Zombies Ate My Mom
Zombies Bought The Farm

* Forthcoming

OCTOBER

MARK FASSETT

RAVENSTAR PRESS
MONROE, WA

Published 2015 by Ravenstar Press
Monroe, WA
http://www.ravenstarpress.com

Designed by Ravenstar Press
Cover Design by Ravenstar Press

Cover Photograph
© Dmytro Konstantynov | Dreamstime.com

ISBN: 978-0692388624

Visit http://markfassett.com/newsletter to join Mark's mailing list and get notified about his newest releases.

ACKNOWLEDGEMENTS

As always, this book would not be the same without the help of a number of people, many of whom don't even know they helped.

Kendra Harrington, Michael Kingswood, Rebecca M. Senese, Michael Canfield, and Jeff Ambrose all provided insights and timely nit-picks. My wife and kids gave me all the support that could be expected, and even some that wasn't.

ONE

It's a terrible thing to wake from a slumber, the sleep still in your eyes, to find your lover no longer by your side.

When I think back, I remember the long night of watered down drinks (for her) and distant conversation. What I can't remember is doing anything to cause her to leave me the next morning.

At first glance, it was like any other morning when she went to work. She had made her side of the bed while I slept. She even left a bagel and cream cheese and a pot of coffee brewing for me for breakfast. We had been living together for a couple years at that point, and we had fallen into a routine that she had followed to the letter. There was nothing different that would have led me to think she had left.

Except that she smelled gone.

There was an emptiness in the apartment that hadn't been there before, and it was palpable.

I don't think I realized it, though, until I poured myself a cup of coffee, spread the cream cheese on the bagel, sat down at the bar stool in the kitchen, and tasted the first bitter drop of coffee to cross my tongue. It tasted like absence.

I looked up, examined the living room, saw the knickknacks we had purchased together still sitting on the shelf next to the television. Except the picture she had of her mother which normally stood next to the crystal turtle we had found in some tiny shop on one of our trips. The picture was missing. The turtle remained.

My ivory Eclipse electric guitar sat next to the shelf, unused in the year since I had left my last band, mocking me in its loneliness. Candi had said that it didn't matter that I had left, that she stood by me, and would continue to stand by me until I found another gig. But the band had planted a sour seed deep within me, and even the idea of looking for another gig had become painful.

The walls were empty, where they had once been covered in posters, gold and platinum records, and other memorabilia from the band. I had taken it all down the day after I quit, claiming to Candi that I was doing it to make room for my next life.

Candi had even tried to put up a painting to bring some life to the room, but I had stopped her. I don't even know why I stopped her. Maybe it was that those walls were reserved for my accomplishments. Maybe they just reminded me of my failure. Maybe I hoped they would inspire me to some new success.

Once Candi was gone, they only looked more empty—a blank canvas, and I had no paint.

But she *had* left the knickknacks. A sign that she might come back.

About a week after she left, when I hadn't heard from

her and she hadn't returned any of my calls, I realized she wasn't coming back and wasn't going to pay her portion of the rent. I found myself looking at my bank account, which had dwindled to the point where it would pay, perhaps, three months' rent. That was if I didn't buy food, pay for power, or even take a shower. A measly six thousand dollars wouldn't last long at all in downtown Seattle.

I swore, sitting there in the chair in front of my computer, there had been over a hundred thousand in the account just a few months earlier. I couldn't recall, either, where it had gone. I knew we had thrown a few parties, and we took that trip to Miami, but it couldn't have gone that quick.

I scrolled down through the history, checked every transaction, added them up. After fifteen minutes of that, I gave up. The numbers didn't lie, even though I still didn't think we had spent all that money. But we had. Or maybe...

No. She hadn't spent it on her own.

I'd spent it on her.

And when she realized it was almost gone, realized I wasn't bringing in any more, she just left. No dramatics, no arguments. She just moved on.

My doorbell, a deep sounding thromb, echoed throughout the apartment.

I closed my eyes and tried to remember if I was supposed to see anyone. I couldn't remember having scheduled anything. I turned to ask Candi, because she always remembered...

Right.

She wasn't there.

The thromb rung again.

"Fuck, I'm coming," I said, though not particularly loudly. It might be someone I didn't want to offend.

I got up from the computer, brushed my hand down my chest, and realized I was shirtless.

I looked down.

Underwear only, black, and in need of a wash.

And Candi wasn't there to do it.

I decided I'd wash them later.

I walked down the short hallway to the door and looked through the peephole.

On the other side of the door, standing heavily in a worn leather coat, was my friend and sometimes manager, Mike. It was hard to tell through the peephole whether his hair was wet, or just especially greasy, but it hung in thick strands to fall below his shoulders, framing the short, but thick, beard he had worn since I'd first met him.

I opened the door.

"What do you want?" I asked, feigning indignation. It wasn't hard, as I didn't exactly want to see him right that moment, but his company would be better than the emptiness I'd endured since Candi left.

Mike put his hand up in front of his face.

"Jesus, dude! Put some clothes on! It's afternoon, already."

"Shit, is it?" I asked.

"Yeah," he said and pushed past me into the living room with his head turned away from me. "It's near three o'clock."

I shut the door, and then followed him in, wondering how I had lost track of so many hours. I could have sworn that it was only ten AM.

A black t-shirt, free of any designs, lay on the couch. I picked it up and pulled it on. A pair of black exercise shorts lay on the floor, and I bent down and picked them up.

"Clean clothes?" Mike asked.

"These are clean...ish," I said.

"You wore them yesterday," he said.

"I had them on earlier." I wasn't going to confirm that I hadn't had them on since yesterday.

"You weren't sitting here watching porn, were you?"

I pointed at the computer screen and its dry, yet dire, proclamation regarding my finances. I didn't give a shit if he learned how bad off I was. He knew all my secrets.

"Unless you think bank statements are porn..."

He didn't look long at the screen before he wandered over and sat down on the couch, away from where the t-shirt had lain.

"Dude, you've got to get your shit together."

I couldn't tell if the statement was in reference to the numbers on the screen, or to something else.

I sat down in the computer chair and spun around to face him.

"I'm fine," I said.

"Bullshit. When was the last time you left this place and went out?"

"Last night," I lied. "I went and got pizza."

He glanced over his shoulder at the counter where the pizza box was sitting, half open. Beside it, a pile of take-out boxes from other restaurants collected over several previous nights crowded the counter-top.

"Like hell you did. You had it delivered. You haven't been out of this place since she left, have you?"

I looked away and my eyes caught the picture of Candi's mom. I could see Candi in her face, the dark eyes, the sharp bones of her cheeks.

"Jesus, dude. You've still got pictures of her mom hanging around? I would have chucked that shit first thing."

"She might come back for it."

"Have you heard from her?"

"No."

"She isn't coming back for it."

I knew that. Still, I didn't even want to think that. My silence on the matter apparently bothered him, as he looked around the room, pausing on every item that Candi had left behind.

After he was done, he returned his gaze to me.

"She left all this shit behind. You're sure she just left?"

"Yeah," I said.

"She leave a note or something? She tell you she was leaving?"

"No, but I tried to call her at work. Someone else answered the phone, then passed me on to her boss." I looked out the window but didn't actually look at anything beyond it. "She told me that Candi had been transferred to the Denver office."

"And Candi didn't tell you? Dude, she's not coming back."

"I know, but she might."

Mike snorted, but he didn't say anything.

Instead, he stood up and went over to my guitar and picked it up. He put the strap over his shoulder—he's a bigger guy than me, and the guitar rode high on him, but he didn't adjust it.

I didn't like that he was holding it. It was my baby, it was what I had used to bring me whatever success I had had.

Mike strummed a chord, and the steel strings jangled, completely out of tune.

He looked up at me.

"Dude, when was the last time you played this thing?"

"I don't know," I said. "It's been awhile."

"I'd say," he said, and then started tuning it.

When he was satisfied, he strummed a chord again, and even without the amplifier to explode the full body of the sound of the guitar, the tone was still discernible, still sweet.

"Better," Mike said.

He took the guitar off and set it back on its stand, as if sensing my unease and giving in to it.

"Why are you here, Mike?"

He blinked his eyes twice, slowly, pondering my question.

"You're a mess, dude. You haven't played that guitar in months, I'd bet. You insist Candi is coming back when we both know she isn't. This place, you're letting it all go to hell, and you can't even be bothered to put some clothes on before you answer the door."

"Tell me something I don't know," I said, more than a little belligerently.

"Are you drinking again?" he asked.

"No," I said.

I had thought about it. The call of whiskey and vodka had grown stronger since Candi left, but I hadn't given in. I hadn't left the apartment, which was probably the only reason I was still sober. There wasn't anything in the apartment to drink.

"Well, that's something, I guess."

I didn't like his superior tone, and I tired of the grilling he was giving me.

"I know all the shit I'm in, Mike. I know I'm fucked up right now. Why the fuck are you here?"

"You swear you're sober, that if I offered you a gig, you could stay sober?"

"A gig? I don't want charity," I said.

"It's not charity," he said. "I swear."

"Then what is it?" I asked.

"You swear you can stay sober?"

"I swear," I said. "That shit ruined Narcoleptic Souls, and I'm not going to let that happen again. You know I was sober for the entire time with Savage Anarchy."

"I know. I just had to be sure. Your apartment looks like it did when you were drinking, just without the bottles. I wasn't even sure if I offered you a gig, that you'd take it."

"You still haven't told me what it is. I might not take it." I don't know why I was so insistent that he tell me what it was. I still didn't really want a gig. It was only my glance at my bank account that morning that caused me to have any interest at all. But if I was going to have to work to find out what it was, Mike was going to piss me off.

I determined that if he didn't tell me in the next few seconds, I'd tell him no, just on the principal of not wanting to be fucked with.

"It's just two nights and a couple of rehearsals," he said. "A fill-in at The Showcase."

"The Showcase? That's what you've got for me? I haven't played a place like that since I was sixteen. I thought you said it was a gig."

He didn't get agitated like I expected. He had probably anticipated my reaction.

"The place is under new ownership," he said. "You've been away from the local scene for awhile. They actually book acts, these days. They don't do the whole talent show thing anymore."

I leaned back in my chair. He was right. I had been away. World tours in arenas, followed by hiding in my apartment except for the times when I went to parties. I'd avoided anything that even resembled live music.

He'd given me enough information to keep from kicking him out. Two nights, a fill-in. Nothing permanent. But he was still coy about the whole thing.

"Who is it?" I asked.

"Three thousand bucks for the two nights," he said.

"You're kidding," I said, forgetting about who it was for the moment. "No one playing club shows pays that much for a fill-in."

"They asked specifically for you," he said.

"Who?"

"Do you want the gig? They didn't want me to tell you who it was until you took it."

I stood up, walked around the couch and into the kitchen. I opened the refrigerator and stood there, staring at the contents.

Three thousand bucks, and they didn't want me to know who they were. That could only mean they thought I wouldn't take the gig if I knew. I had ideas, people who I had had words with over the years. Bands that felt we had slighted them on our rise up.

The other option, of course, was that it was a band that was up-and-coming, but no one knew, and thought the only way I would play for them was if they offered enough money.

I shut the refrigerator. My answers weren't in there. The beer I felt like I needed, but didn't really want, wasn't there, either. I wasn't lying to him. I hadn't started drinking again.

"Who is it? Is it someone I don't like? If I say yes, and then I get there, and find out I can't stand them, I'll leave, no matter what the money is like."

"You don't know them," Mike said from his seat on the couch. He didn't even turn to face me.

"Then how are they offering that much? It's a ridiculous amount of money for a two night gig at a club."

But three thousand bucks would help me out.

Mike pushed himself up out of the couch.

"Look, do you care how they're offering that much? The money is on the table if you show up for rehearsals on Wednesday and Thursday, then the shows on Friday and Saturday. Personally, I think you need this. Get your head back in it. Do something productive. I know you need the money, and I bet you need something to kick-start you again. You're too damned good a player to be sitting on the couch letting your fingers rot."

I looked up at the ceiling, stared down the smooth, pearl white paint. Eventually, I let my gaze fall down to look at Mike, who was patiently waiting for my answer. Behind him, my empty wall stood, lending his argument weight that it didn't really need.

"Fine, I'll be there. Can you at least tell me the style of music?"

Mike smiled.

"I think you'll like it. And hell, if you don't, it's only a week."

He handed me a piece of paper, then turned and headed for the door.

"Where you going?" I asked.

"I've got things to do. I'll see you at the rehearsal studio, Wednesday at noon."

I looked at the paper he'd given me. It had an address on it. He'd expected me to take it, if he offered it.

"You're going to be there?"

"Of course," he said. He looked at me and smiled, his bearded face lighting up with the mischievous grin. "I promised them I'd keep an eye on you."

He walked down the hallway without another word, then I heard the door open and shut.

Fuck.

I'd just agreed to play, and I had two days to get back into shape before I showed up at that rehearsal.

I looked at my guitar.

I stretched my fingers and imagined the steel strings underneath my fingertips. It was going to hurt.

But I had agreed, and I wasn't going to go to that rehearsal cold.

I still had some pride.

TWO

It probably didn't matter that, in the days leading up to Candi leaving me, we hadn't spoken much. She was working, I was busy not working. She was tired, she said, and I took her at her word. What else was I to do?

I was oblivious, ignoring the world around me even as I pretended to live in it.

The pain in the pads of my fingers that came from sliding them up and down the guitar strings for the first time in a year was all it took to prove it to me. My fingers hurt like hell, and I loved it.

If I was only a casual player and spent only a half-hour or so practicing, my fingers would have been fine.

But I still had some pride in my ability, and the first half hour only proved to me how far out of practice I was.

I spent four hours the first day just working on my scales and chord switches, trying to get back as much of my speed as possible. I knew it wasn't going to come all in one day, but I worked as if it would.

I tried to take breaks every half hour to rest my fingers, but even so, I had to quit before I wanted to because the pain was too much. I needed to give my fingers time to heal, time they didn't have.

And I wasn't even close to being as fast and smooth as I had been a year ago.

And it was frustrating as hell.

I looked at the tips of the fingers on my fretting hand and saw a deep redness where the strings had rubbed against them. There were lines in my fingers.

I was pushing it.

I knew if I pushed it too far, I wouldn't be able to do the gig. There's nothing worse as a guitar player than not being able to push down on the strings because you overworked yourself and gave yourself a cut on your finger. Steel strings and a sliced finger make playing nearly impossible. The sting of it is almost unbearable.

I sat down on my couch with my phone beside me, and stared at my guitar. I glanced at my fingers, then back at the guitar.

"This is your fault," I told it.

It said nothing, though. It wouldn't say a word without my fingers on it.

It wasn't the guitar's fault at all.

I picked up the phone and dialed Mike, but he didn't answer, and I laid the phone back down.

Mike wasn't going to give me a chance to back out. I both approved of his choice and hated him for it at the same time.

"Fuck you, Mike," I said, even though he couldn't hear me.

What I didn't want to admit to myself in that moment was that I had enjoyed playing again. It had taken my mind off of Candi for those four hours as I worked to shake off the rust. I felt better than I had in weeks. Perhaps, better than I had felt since I quit playing a year ago.

The next morning, when I woke, I went right to my guitar, picked it up, and started to play.

My fingers still hurt like hell, but I ran through my warm-up exercises, my scales, and a series of chord progressions.

When I finished the warm-ups, I knew I wouldn't be able to practice as much as I had the previous day, but my fingering felt smoother, which was a bit of progress.

I had to quit after an hour. My fingertips wouldn't take any more, and I didn't want to risk splitting them open. I didn't want to quit. Again, thoughts of Candi disappeared in the effort to make my fingers work again, and reappeared soon after.

I examined my fingers. The redness was even darker than the day before. I didn't think they'd heal before the end of the gig, but if I managed it correctly, they'd at least last. I wouldn't be my old self on the guitar, but I had to hope that Mike had taken that into account. He knew I hadn't been playing.

I put the guitar away, resolving to come back to it later in the day for another hour.

I found my phone and dialed Mike again.

This time, he picked up.

"Hey," he said. "How's it going?"

"My fingers hurt like a bitch," I said.

"Good, good. I was hoping to hear something like that. You back to your old self?"

"No," I said. "I don't think I'll embarrass myself, but I won't be shredding it all night, either."

"Don't worry, you won't need to. It should be an easy gig."

I rolled my eyes back in my head, even though I knew he wouldn't be able to see them.

"Easy?"

"Yeah, you know the songs, mostly."

"Can you send me a set list?"

He laughed.

"Nice try, but you're not going to get a chance to back out until after you show up."

"You think I'll back out if I know the set list?"

"I think that if you knew, you'd make guesses about the band that would be incorrect and back out. I don't want that to happen. I worked too hard to set this up."

"You're an asshole," I said. I could feel myself smiling, though.

"I'm only watching out for you, brother. Be there tomorrow, go through a rehearsal with them. If you want to back out then, be my guest. At least give it a chance."

"You don't have to worry," I said, wondering if I was lying to him. "I'm committed to the weekend. The money is enough to see to that."

"Good," he said. "I'll see you tomorrow."

He hung up.

And I still had the rest of the day to worry about tomorrow while nursing fingers that wanted to play but needed to rest. I had all day to think about Candi and wonder where she was.

THREE

I stood out back of a two-story brick building that had all the earmarks of having been built fifty years earlier with some fine masonry work that now needed a lot of love. The windows of the first floor sported iron bars, and most were blacked out. A small sign to the left of the electronically-locked steel door said *Blue Mountain Rehearsal Studios* in delicate, hand lettered, calligraphy. The door was locked, and Mike hadn't given me the key code to get in.

I glanced back at the plain white van I used to transport my gear. I had parked it in a small parking lot behind the building, taking the last stall. I carried only my guitar with me to the door, hoping that they had an amp I could play through. My own rig was far too big and too much of a pain in the ass for me to want to get it out just for a rehearsal. I hoped it would be all right. The neighborhood didn't seem too shifty, but you never knew. I just hoped that the fact the van had no markings would keep it safe.

That was the whole point of not marking it. I probably should have put an ad for a plumber on it.

The muffled sound of music being played seeped out through the cracks in the walls and windows of the building. There had to be at least three bands inside. Knocking was of no use.

I pulled my phone out of my pocket and checked the time.

Mike had said to be at the door at ten in the morning, and that they had a four hour window in which to get the rehearsal done. I was early by a few minutes, but I had at least expected Mike to be there to introduce me to the band.

I closed my eyes and took a deep breath, then let it out slowly.

"Mike will be here," I said. "I'm just early."

Repeating the idea out loud gave it more power to calm my nerves.

I was wired.

Fuck me for being early. I should have played the rock star and been late, if just by a few minutes. Enough to be sure that Mike was here and that I wouldn't be standing out back of a locked rehearsal studio like a chump.

I heard a car pull in to the parking lot, and I opened my eyes.

It was a tiny Kia something or other, black, economy wheels, and tinted windows. Music thumped out through the car's thin walls—the owner spent more money on the sound system, I would bet, than they did on the car. Heavy music, thumping bass and crunching guitars, the kind of music I preferred to play. Thankfully, it wasn't my old band.

The driver whipped into a parking space so quickly that I couldn't get a look at them through the windshield before they parked.

Whoever it was, it wasn't Mike. Mike only drove German engineering these days.

After a moment of waiting—whoever was behind the wheel, they were apparently going to finish listening to the song before shutting the car off—I realized that this could be one of the band members.

The music and the car shut off.

A few seconds later, the driver got out of the car.

Over the top of the other cars in the parking lot, a blonde-haired head popped up. The hair was cut close, but I could only see the back. I couldn't make out a face.

And then the head turned to face me, and I saw it was a girl, well, older than a girl, but certainly not any older than her early twenties. She wasn't wearing a whole lot of makeup, but her eyes still looked large and dark, deep pools I could fall into. Her hair was bleached, I now saw, as evidenced by her dark eyebrows.

She grinned as she looked at me, then waived.

I waived back, absently. I was far more interested in how hard my heart pounded within my chest.

I told myself it was nerves, just nerves. In a few minutes, I would be playing with a group, again.

She bounced out from behind her car, wearing a cut-to-shreds black tank top that still managed to hide the important parts and black leggings that clung to every curve of her legs. Her calf-high leather boots had to have springs in them, as the three inch heels on them could not have allowed her to bounce as much as she seemed to be doing. She was giddy as all hell.

"I hope to hell you didn't hook me up with a bunch of fanboys, Mike," I said under my breath. I still wasn't in any sort of mental shape to deal with the fawning that always came along with them.

Unfortunately, Mike still wasn't there to answer the question. I knew I'd have to put up with whatever he'd done, at least until he arrived.

The girl seemed to calm herself down as she approached me.

"You must be Trent," she said, her giddiness only slightly evident in her voice.

I hoped I kept the shock off my face. I had thought she already knew me, that she was groupie material, but her first words put that to rest a little. She could be pretending.

"I am," I said. "You are?"

"Elise. Mike said you were cute." I'll give her credit. She didn't blush as she said it. Her eyes sparkled, instead.

"Wait... You don't know who I am?"

"You're Trent Richards, right?"

"Yes."

"Then you're the guitar player that Mike sent to help us out. That's all I know, I swear."

The guitar player. What kind of game was he playing?

"Mike told me you asked for me by name," I said.

Elise smiled, and leaned in to me conspiratorially. "Nope. We just asked him if he knew any guitar players that could help us out, with the requirement that male guitar players had to be cute."

Then she stuck her hand past me and tapped the keypad a few times.

She hadn't been leaning in conspiratorially. She was just letting us in.

"And you're definitely cute," she said with a smile.

The door latch clicked open.

"Come on, let's talk inside," she said. "The rehearsal space is way more comfortable."

Then she bounced past me and into a dimly lit hallway. I guess giddiness was her natural state.

I followed after her.

She led me past a half a dozen closed doors, some of which were obviously occupied. The sound proofing was not enough to keep in all the noise. And some of it *was* just noise.

About half way down the hallway, Elise turned to the right down another hallway, and walked all the way to the end. She unlocked a scarred door on the right and stepped inside.

I followed her through, and she let the door shut behind us.

The room was a pretty good size, I guessed twenty-five feet to a side, with a raised floor on the far end that served as a stage. A nondescript drum kit was set up on the stage in the center with a couple of beat up amplifiers flanking it. An electric piano stood stage left, and three microphone stands lined the front of the stage.

Bass, drums, keyboard, one guitar, maybe two. Pretty standard rock lineup.

I glanced to my right and saw a plush bright-pink couch that was as big a couch as I had ever seen. It would have fit half a dozen people on it, and you could still get lost in all the pink. I know it probably says something about me, but I didn't want to get caught sitting on that couch. I looked to my left, hoping to see a place to sit that was not so bright, and found only a beat up equipment crate, the black plastic adorned with spray-painted pink hearts.

All in all, ignoring the couch, the room wasn't too bad as far as budget rehearsal rooms go. I'd been in worse. This one didn't stink of beer or cigarette smoke, though there was a vague hint of perfume-covered sweat.

"You have exclusive use of the room?" I asked.

"Yeah. We shared the last one, and figure we lost more money in busted equipment and wasted time than we spend renting this place out. Plus, we can come and go as we want."

I pointed to the stage. "Which amp do I use?"

"Oh, the one on the right. You're taking Jan's place."

Jan.

"Jan? How many girls are in this group?"

She laughed. "I guess Mike didn't tell you much about us. We're *all* girls."

I gestured toward the pink couch.

"I guess that explains the couch. I'm beginning to wonder if I'm the right guy for this gig."

She walked over and stood right in front of me, looking up slightly to capture my eyes.

"Look, Mike said you can do this, and we trust him. We didn't put an all girl band together on purpose. It just worked out that way."

"Yeah, but..."

She poked me in the chest with an extended fingernail.

"Just wait until you hear us before you make any judgments. We haven't heard you, either, you know."

"You know," I said as I stared down into her probing eyes, "you probably have."

This close, I could definitely see she couldn't be any older than twenty-three. There was too much bubbly innocence in her eyes. I felt like I could see through them to her soul, and there wasn't any pain in it.

Of course, that couldn't be true. Everyone had pain. I'd learned that the hard way. Maybe it was just my luck that I couldn't see it in people if it wasn't right on the surface, exposed by drugs or drink or a flaw in the person's character—like with Candi and how I never saw her leaving. On the surface, things were good.

I turned away, unable to continue to look at Elise any longer, and strode to the right side of the stage. I set my guitar case on the floor in front of the stage and opened it up.

"That's beautiful," Elise said from behind me.

I felt her bending over me, but I refused to look up at her. "It is, isn't it?"

The ivory color had a translucent quality that gave it some depth. Maybe it was just the clear coat, but it really did seem that you could look three inches deep into the paint.

"It almost doesn't look like it's been played," she said. I could hear the hidden question in her statement.

I reached into the case and picked up the guitar.

"It's been played," I said, not quite understanding why I was answering the hidden question. "I had it restored right after I left my last band, sort of as a present for finally making the decision to leave." And also as a way to wash away the memory of the experience.

She didn't need to know that the last couple days were the most I'd played it since I restored it. She didn't need to know it sat unused for more than a year.

"Nice present," she said.

I felt her stand up, and I stood up with the guitar and strapped it on before turning to face her.

She wasn't looking at me, she was looking at the guitar. It was obvious she appreciated it.

"You want to try it?" I asked, making as if I would take it off.

She smiled and looked up from the guitar.

"No, no. I don't play, though I've always sort of wanted to."

"Then what do you do?" I asked.

"I sing, and I write lyrics," she said.

I couldn't imagine what kind of lyrics her bubbly personality would come up with. Bubble-gum pop, I'd bet.

I shut my eyes tight, and told myself to calm down. It wasn't fair to judge her, or the band. They did what they did, whatever that was, and they had a gig. Whatever happened here, it was Mike's fault, if the fault belonged to anyone.

"You all right?" Elise asked.

"Yeah, yeah. I'm fine." I opened my eyes and was met with a worried gaze from her. "It's just that I just expected Mike to be here to help me through this, or at least to introduce us. I've been through some..." Her eyes started to grow more worried, or worse, sympathetic. "Hell, it doesn't matter. I'm guessing I have a pile of music to learn in three days. We should probably get to it."

I grabbed the cable from my guitar case and went over to the amp to plug in. She stood where I left her. When I looked back, I could see the curiosity in her face, and perhaps a bit more than just bubbles.

Then she took a deep breath.

"Mike did say he would be here a little later," she said. "He didn't want to get in the way."

I chuckled. "Of course he didn't."

I flipped the switch on the amp and waited for it to warm up.

"How soon until the others arrive?" I asked.

"They should be here, soon. Mike thought it would be better if I met you here a little early."

And then it dawned on me.

"Tell me something. Do you have a boyfriend?"

"Not at the moment," and then her eyes went wide as it dawned on her, too.

And then she laughed.

"You think he's trying to set us up?" she asked.

"I think that's exactly what he's trying to do," I said. "You really don't know who I am, do you?"

"No."

"Do the others know?"

"No. Mike told me not to tell them. He said he wanted it to be a surprise."

"You weren't even a little curious? You didn't search for me on the internet?"

"I didn't have time. Mike didn't tell me your name until this morning. He's a sneaky bastard, isn't he?"

I nodded. I heard the hum of the amp behind me, its tubes finally warm, and a pretty decent level already set. My fingers itched to start warming up, but I still had to wrap my head around what Mike was trying to accomplish.

Elise *was* cute enough.

"He's just trying to make sure I don't cut out."

"Why would you cut out?"

"I'd rather not get into it right now, but I swear, I'm good for these shows. I won't leave you guys in the lurch, whatever Mike thinks I might do."

Her smile disappeared, but she wasn't frowning. She looked puzzled, instead, her brow furrowed.

"Well, then, do you want to tell me who you are?"

"How about we wait until the others arrive. Then I can surprise you all at once."

I didn't want to have to go through two separate fangirl reactions within the space of a half-hour. Not that they would do that, but I wanted to minimize the chance.

"Fine," she said with a laugh, but the puzzlement remained.

"I think I'm going to warm up, now, if you don't mind. My fingers are itching to play." And I didn't want this conversation to continue much longer. I needed time to think.

"Go ahead," she said, and turned away.

I started slowly, with limbering up exercises, then worked into my scales. The strings cut into the pads on my fingers, but not nearly as much as they had that first day. I was starting to grow back some of my calluses.

Elise walked over to the pink couch and plunged into its cushions. She reached into her purse, pulled out her cell phone, and started tapping on the screen.

She wasn't going to wait for me to announce my identity, or for the others to show up.

Fine by me.

I kept an eye on her, but directed most of my concentration inward, toward my playing. I finished my scales, and then went into some chord work. A, C, E, all the way up and down the neck. Every permutation I knew. Then the minors, followed by the sevenths, the ninths. When those were done, I started another three chord combination.

I glanced up and saw that Elise was staring at me, her phone on her lap.

I kept working on my warm-up.

She glanced down at her phone, then back up at me. Her mouth didn't exactly fall open, but her lips parted.

She knew.

I saw her lips mouth the words "Holy shit."

I couldn't help but smile.

But I also couldn't help but be worried. This was exactly the kind of reaction I had hoped wouldn't happen.

I had drilled it into myself after Candi left.

No more star-struck girlfriends, no matter how much I liked them.

FOUR

The others showed up not ten minutes later, while I was playing through bits and pieces of songs that I used to get my rhythm in sync.

The first, a tall brunette wearing a pink sweat suit and her hair back in a ponytail, looked like she had jogged her way to the rehearsal studio. She had sweat on her face and a towel in her right hand. A particularly large drop of sweat fell from the point of a long, but thin, nose as she noticed me for the first time.

She cocked her head to the left, then glanced at the couch where Elise was sitting.

Elise waved, then got up from the couch.

I kept playing. I was almost done with my warm-up and I didn't want to stop before I finished.

The two women converged and hugged each other. The brunette bent her head down to Elise's ear and said something that I couldn't hear over the guitar. Elise nodded, then said something back to the brunette, before they both turned and looked at me.

I smiled, but kept playing.

The brunette bent to Elise's ear and said one more thing, then hugged her before leaving Elise to walk over to the electric piano.

Which answered one question. She was the keyboard player.

A minute later, she had the keyboard on, and then started playing along with the song I was playing, an old Nirvana song. It meant I had to finish the song instead of switching up, but it was probably just as valuable to play with someone as to warm up alone.

Within three bars, I knew she was good, too.

At the start of the second verse, two other women walked into the room, clearly twins. They both had jet black hair that hung to their shoulders, the same delicately blunt nose, dark brown eyes and round, soft cheeks. They dressed differently, however. One wore jeans and a Nine Inch Nails shirt, and had a tiny diamond on her nose. The other wore a tight black skirt that stopped just short of her knees, a white blouse, and pink suspenders. She had earrings that dangled nearly to her shoulders, but did not have anything adorning her nose.

The one with the nose ring frowned when she saw me, but the other grew a huge smile and practically jumped up and down in excitement. It was clear they both knew who I was.

I looked at my unnamed piano player, and we cut off the song.

The music died out, and for a moment, there was silence in the room.

Pink suspenders said, "Elise, you didn't tell us our sub would be Trent Richards!" She didn't even turn toward Elise, but continued to stare at me.

"No," nose ring said. "You didn't. I'm not sure he's a good fit."

Elise went over to the two women, embraced them in one combined hug.

"I didn't know until this morning, and even then, I didn't know him by name. And Rose, I think he's perfect."

Rose must be the one with the nose ring.

"You would," Rose said, disengaging herself from the hug.

Pink suspenders also disengaged from the hug, but instead of just standing in the doorway, she nearly ran across the room and stuck her hand out to me.

"Hi, I'm Adelle," she said. "I just loved your work with Savage Anarchy!"

"Hey," I said, taking her hand. It was moist with instant, nervous, perspiration. "I'm Trent."

"I can't believe you're going to be playing with us."

"I'm just a guitar player," I said.

She giggled. "Yeah, right. My boyfriend will be so surprised."

Well, that settled that. I didn't have to worry so much about Adelle. Just an excited fan, which was okay.

"If I was guessing, I'd have to say you play the bass," I said in an attempt to change the conversation. I based my guess on the differences between her and her sister. I figured her sister for the beat-the-shit-out-of-the-drums kind of girl.

"Nah, that's Rose. I'm the drummer."

"Ah, sorry. I'm no good at guessing that kind of shit."

"That's all right. It happens all the time. No one thinks that someone who likes to dress nice would play the drums, especially not a girl."

And then there was an awkward silence between us.

"He ruins bands!" Rose shouted into that silence.

I looked up, and Adelle turned around. Elise had a shocked look on her face, and Rose looked angry. Her finger was pointed straight at me.

"Rose! You take that back," Adelle said.

Rose looked at Adelle.

"I'm not taking anything back. Everyone knows his alcoholism destroyed Narcoleptic Souls, and while no one ever said anything, who's to say it wasn't the same thing that caused him to leave Savage Anarchy?"

The room went silent.

I went cold.

They were all looking at me, waiting for me to respond, waiting for me to say something.

A hundred different responses ran through my head. Everything from "Fuck you" to "I don't need this shit" to "You don't deserve to know the answer, bitch." I kept them all in my head, though. What I really wanted to know was why it even mattered. It was just a weekend gig. Hard to fuck up a band that much in a weekend.

But as coy as Mike had been, I couldn't help think that there was more going on here than I knew. Like perhaps that this was more than just a weekend gig.

"Fuck this," I said.

I took my guitar from my shoulder and went to put it away, pulling the cord from the amp as I left the stage.

Elise ran toward me, panic on her face.

"Please, please. She didn't mean it."

I set the guitar into the case, then looked up and started coiling up the cord.

Across the room, Rose's face was set, hard, waiting for me to say something. She had her hands on her hips.

"She meant it," I said. "I don't know what her deal is, but it isn't worth the money for the weekend to put up with that kind of shit. I've had enough hostility in bands to last me a lifetime. I don't need some high and mighty bitch questioning me about shit that happened years ago. Not for a weekend gig. Not for anything."

I wrapped up the last bit of the cord and set it in my guitar case, then shut the lid and latched it.

"What do you mean about a weekend gig?" Elise asked at the same time that Rose started to huff and snort.

"We're well rid of you," Rose said. "We don't need ass-holes like you."

Elise turned to Rose.

"Shut up, Rose!" she shouted.

Rose's eyes opened wide, apparently surprised that Elise had shouted at her. If I had been in any other mood, it might have even been funny.

She didn't say anything, though.

Elise turned back to me. I already had my guitar case in my hand, ready to walk.

She put a hand on my chest to keep me from going anywhere.

"Trent. Tell me what you meant by 'a weekend gig'."

"That's what this is, isn't it? That's what Mike told me."

She shook her head.

"No. I mean, yes, it's a weekend gig, but it's more than that. If it works out, it's a place in the band."

"Fucking Mike, that bastard..."

The words had barely escaped my mouth when the door opened behind Rose and Mike walked in.

"What about that bastard?" Mike asked with a smile on his face.

He had heard me.

I stepped around Elise and off the stage, then walked right past Rose so that I could speak to Mike face to face.

"You lied to me," I said. "You told me this was just the weekend."

"You're right. I did lie to you. Would you have come if I had told you otherwise?"

"Fuck no, I don't want to be in a band anymore. I'm tired of the politics." I pointed at Rose. "Not thirty seconds after she walks in the door, she's already grilling me about Savage Anarchy. I'm done with this shit."

I stepped around him and walked out the door before he could answer.

I stalked down the hall, ignoring Mike as he called after me.

What really sucked is that, for that couple of minutes playing along with the keyboard player whose name I still didn't know, it had felt good making music again. It was just fun.

And Rose had come in and ruined it.

No. That wasn't fair to her. Not really.

Mike ruined it by tricking me into the gig, and not telling them who he had found to replace Jan. He was playing the games.

I stepped out into the parking lot, letting the door shut behind me. I heard the lock click. There was no getting back in.

Which was probably for the better, because, as I started to calm down and thought over what happened, I realized that it wasn't all Rose's fault. It was Mike's. He had set up the disaster.

And I liked Elise.

I felt bad about walking out on her, even after telling her I wouldn't leave her in the lurch for the weekend.

I walked across the parking lot to my van, opened the rear doors, shoved my guitar inside. I stood there for a moment with my hand on the door, ready to shut it, but with the cool air helping to clear my head, I climbed in and sat down with my legs dangling out the back, instead.

As I sat there, knowing now that what Mike had in mind was more audition for a spot in the band than weekend fill-in, I realized that Rose's concern was appropriate, given the context. If Mike had told them ahead of time, things might have gone better. But then, maybe they would have decided to not bring me in in the first place. Maybe they would have decided they couldn't take the risk. This way, Mike gets me in, they get the guitar player they need. If I hadn't been so fucking sensitive to Rose's question about my past with both of those bands, then perhaps things would also have gone better. But if I hadn't been so sensitive about that shit, I wouldn't have needed Mike's help, either.

"Oh well," I said aloud so that I could hear someone say it. "It's too late, now."

"Too late for what?" Elise asked as she stepped around the open door of the van.

I had apparently missed the sound of the studio door opening and closing.

"I fucked that up royally, didn't I?"

"I don't know. Mike's in there apologizing to everyone, pleading for them to give you a chance."

"And you're out here. I would have expected Mike."

She smiled. "He's got bigger problems. Rose wants to fire him."

"I want to fire him, too," I said. But I couldn't. We'd been friends too long. "Why are you out here?"

"To try to convince you to come back in."

"Does Rose want that?"

"I don't care. I heard you play with Carol. You're an incredible player. We have to have you, even if it's only for this weekend. We'll have to cancel the shows if you don't help us."

"I don't want to deal with the hostility. I left Savage Anarchy because of the people, not because I was drinking. I don't want to deal with negative people anymore."

"Rose isn't normally negative. She just cares a lot about the band. It's what she lives for."

I had been that way, once, right after I became sober. I had replaced drinking with Savage Anarchy. Leaving still hurt, just thinking about it.

"Are you sure she'll be okay?"

"I promise," she said. "Please, at least for this weekend?"

I thought about it for long moments, breathing in slowly, breathing out deeply, just trying to settle myself within myself. I could do it for the weekend, and I *did* need the money. I did my best to look at anything other than her sparkling eyes, knowing that just looking would decide me.

I really didn't want the drama.

She started singing, quietly, a sweet little lullaby. Her voice was pure.

> *It'll all be better,*
> *in the morning.*
> *You'll see*
> *You'll see*

Between her eyes and her voice, I couldn't say no.

"For you, just for this weekend. I'm not really looking to join a band right now."

She smiled and her eyes sparkled again. She reached out and took my hand.

"Thank you," she said. "Grab your guitar and let's go back in."

Her smile was impossible to resist.

FIVE

"We good to go?" Mike asked as Elise and I walked into the room.

I avoided looking at him as I responded.

"Yeah, I'm good."

The trip outside and Elise's little song had calmed me, and I didn't want to leave that state. I'd talk with Mike later about what I thought of his stunt.

Instead, I sought out Rose, who was standing with a bright pink bass guitar in her hand that completely clashed with her outfit. Rose's mood had improved, somewhat, as gauged by the fact that she didn't immediately start shouting at me when I returned.

I set my guitar down and climbed up on the stage so that I could talk to Rose quietly. They'd probably all overhear, but I wanted to speak more intimately with her than shouting across a room.

"Hey," I said.

She turned a little to look me in the eye.

"Hey."

The two of us stood quietly for a moment, waiting for the other to say something more. I didn't look away from her, but I could tell everyone else was listening, too, waiting along with us for the ice to break, or for an explosion.

Eventually, I decided I'd go first, seeing as how I should have just explained the situation instead of getting wound up about it.

"I'm sorry," I said, "the wounds are still raw from that experience. I shouldn't have taken your questioning so hard."

Where Elise's eyes were all sparkles and brightness, Rose's eyes were deep pools with dark currents flowing through them. I couldn't figure out what she was thinking.

"Mike explained it. You're sober?"

She wasn't warming up to me.

"Yes."

"You were sober while you were with Savage Anarchy?"

"I was."

"Then get your guitar out. Let's see if you can still play."

We stood silently for another moment, looking at each other. I couldn't believe how she had just said what she said, as if I was nobody.

"I..." I said. My mouth couldn't form the next word, perhaps because my brain couldn't settle on one.

"What?"

There's always one person in charge of a band, no matter how democratic things may seem. There's always one person who wants it more, who directs things and makes sure shit gets done. I had been that person once, with Narcoleptic Souls, before my alcoholism destroyed it. I ended up not getting along with that person in Savage Anarchy.

Rose was that person for this band.

And I had to call her a high and mighty bitch on the first day.

"Right," I said.

I turned away from her, closed my eyes for half a second, breathed in, let it out slowly, then walked across the stage to my guitar case.

A minute later, I had the guitar out, plugged in, and the amp warming up again.

Elise, in the meantime, had bounded up onto the stage, and the others took their places. The PA board sat right at Elise's feet, and she flicked it on with the tip of her shoe.

On the far side of the room, Mike sat down on the couch, pulled out his phone, and started tapping away at it.

"What's first?" I asked, trusting that Mike knew what he was talking about when he told me I would know most of the songs. It led me to assume they were a cover band.

Rose, on the far side of Elise, donned a mischievous grin before she answered me.

"*Rise Above Anger,*" she said.

Adelle counted off the start of the song with four clicks of her drumsticks in rapid-fire succession, and the rest of the band went right into the song without thinking.

I just sat there, dumbfounded.

I turned and looked at Mike, who I discovered had paused in his phone tapping to watch my reaction.

My heart pounded heavy in my chest.

The song was *mine!* One of the last songs I wrote with Narcoleptic Souls.

My chest grew tight.

I hadn't listened to the song, or even any of those albums, in years. Not since I got sober. I haven't even played them since the band collapsed. Not one note.

The band noticed I wasn't playing, and came to a stop.

"What the fuck, Mike!" I shouted.

The shouting helped a little.

"What?" he asked.

"You planned this! You knew they would play this song!"

Mike stood up, shoved the phone in his pocket, and walked my way.

"I did know," he said. "They mostly cover Narc Souls songs, and add in a few of their own."

I really wanted to jam my guitar neck down his throat, right then, but I restrained myself. I forced myself to breathe slowly and deeply, once, before I responded.

"Then why did you think I'd be cool with this?"

"I didn't," he said. "I thought it would be good for you."

"You're an asshole, Mike. Why didn't you ask me, first?"

"You wouldn't have come, and you know it. You *need* this. You've been sitting in that apartment for a year, or more, not once touching your guitar. That thing, it used to be what you lived and breathed. Whatever happened in Savage Anarchy, you were always better in Narc Souls, even with the drinking. The songs, they still get played. People love them. You loved them. Just give it a chance."

"But..."

I couldn't say much more. Just hearing the name of the song took me back to that time. The music, playing it, would force me there, and I couldn't guarantee I could handle that. I had put so much emotion into those songs, so much of myself, that I worried that playing them, or even listening to them, would just bring out that side of me again. I worried that I would not be able to resist the urge to drink again.

Mike stepped up onto the stage and put his hands on my shoulders.

"I know what you're thinking, but I swear to you, that won't happen. You'll be fine. I know you will. You promised me, before I asked, that you were sober. I had to make sure, because I knew what this might do if you weren't."

"And what if this makes me fall off?" I asked in a whisper. Underneath his hands, I could feel myself shaking. "What if it's the songs that caused my problems?"

"The songs didn't cause your problems. They didn't make you drink. You need to play them to see that for yourself."

I knew, logically, that Mike had to be right. But the fear that my sobriety and the fact that I hadn't played those songs since hopping on the wagon were linked had a grip on my gut that wouldn't let go. It was too much to risk.

"I don't want to," I said in a whisper.

"How about this," Mike said. "Play the one song. If you play the one song and you want to quit after that, I'll understand. I'll even help you find another gig you can do to make the money you need. But I want you to play *Rise* for me. And if you're so pissed at me for bringing you here, do it for them."

He swung his arm around like a ring-master at a circus, indicating the girls in the band.

I couldn't help but follow his gesture.

Elise stood holding the microphone in front of her chest, eyes wide, but slightly downturned at the corners, hoping for me to play, I was sure.

Rose stood with most of her weight on her left leg, slowly tapping with the right toe. She waited for me to bail out.

The keyboard player's look was inscrutable. I knew her name now, thanks to Elise, but we still hadn't been introduced, and that bothered me just a little.

Adelle, behind her drums, looked at me with eyebrows raised, hopeful, willing to forgive anything. I think she was still seeing rock-star me, and not the real me.

My gaze drifted back to Rose, her toe still tapping.

Something about her pricked at the bubble I had built around myself. My instincts told me to flee, that this whole thing was a bad idea, but watching her foot tap tugged at me. She thought I wouldn't do it. She thought, probably, that I couldn't.

Fuck it.

I knew, logically, that he was right, that it wasn't the songs. I shoved my worries into the tiny little prison cell in my heart where I kept everything I didn't want to show the world. I'd let logic rule the day. It wasn't the songs. The alcoholism was its own disease, a disease I had conquered. I could beat all this other shit, too.

I turned to Adelle.

"What are you waiting for?" I asked.

She smiled, then lifted her sticks, crashed them together four times, and I dove into the song, unhindered by my worries.

SIX

A nd fuck Mike for being right, at least for the moment. After the first few bars of the song, I closed my eyes and let my fingers roam over the fretboard like they used to. E Minor, G, A. Simple chords, simple fingerings, but the picking, the rhythm of it, was what made the song what it was.

And the band was good. Rose and Adelle were as tight a rhythm section as I'd played with, possibly because they were sisters. The keyboard player—I already knew she was good, but her rendition of the keyboard part transcended even what I had conceived of when I originally wrote the song.

When Elise's voice broke in, I opened my eyes, shocked at the sound, and almost stopped playing.

She was incredible. She somehow combined a sweet, pure tone with just a hint of rasp that said, "You can love me, but don't fuck with me, or I'll kick your ass." I had wondered how she would pull off singing the Narc Souls

MARK FASSETT

lyrics, considering that the original singer had been male with a deep, crusty voice.

I didn't wonder any longer.

Elise's voice was perfect for the Narc Souls songs.

I must have fumbled a little, because she turned and winked at me. Or perhaps she was just looking for my approval.

She had it.

And I managed to keep playing.

After the first verse, I even managed to close my eyes again.

With every note I played, I expected to be jolted by memories, but they never came. Elise's voice turned the song into something that it had never been, keeping the memories at bay.

My fingers had no trouble remembering, but for that one slip.

By the end of the song, I was breathless, and my heart was beating as if I had just run a race, but it wasn't for fear.

When my fingers came off the fretboard after the last note, my hand trembled.

And that was when the memory came—a memory of how I felt when music had been fun. I remembered why I had started playing in the first place.

I opened my eyes, looked at the others.

Every single one of them had their eyes glued on me.

I glanced at Mike, where he sat on the pink couch.

His jaw hung low, his mouth slightly open, his eyes wider than I had seen.

I wasn't the only one whose heart was racing.

But it wasn't Mike's approval that I needed. It was Rose's.

I shocked myself by even realizing I wanted approval.

But I looked at her, anyway.

I needed to know if she felt what I felt, if she felt what I thought the others were feeling.

Her gaze had softened, somewhat, I thought. She had to have recognized what had just happened.

"Holy shit," Elise said. "That was..."

Magical.

"One song," Rose interrupted. "We've got more work to do."

She was right, too. We had a lot of work to do.

But it was still magical.

"*No Sleep On Sundays,*" she said. "Count it off Adelle."

Another Narc Souls song.

Elise glanced at Rose as if she were going to protest, but a raised eyebrow from Rose silenced anything Elise might have wanted to say.

If this was a challenge, I could live up to it. I could prove to her that I wouldn't be a destructive force.

I didn't let myself think, as Adelle's voice rang out through the room counting "Four, three, two," that I had gone from wanting to leave to wanting to stay so badly I could taste it in the four minutes we played that song.

I set my left hand to the fretboard, closed my eyes, and waited, hoping for the magic to fill me up again.

SEVEN

The magic never came to me again with quite the same force during the rest of the rehearsal. It was always close, though, right around the next chord change, just glimpsed through a perfect note sung by Elise, or a flourish on the keys by the woman whose name I still did not know.

We played through all the Narc Souls songs in their set. On every one of them, I prepared again for an awful feeling, but just like the first, Elise's voice changed it up enough that I couldn't possibly relive ancient memories.

Or, more likely, I had just been so drunk the whole time that the memories weren't as strong as they could have been.

After the Narc Souls songs, things slowed a bit and got tougher as I had to learn their songs. They had recordings that I listened to, and Rose and the keyboard player detailed the chord changes, and we somehow worked our way through the songs, one at a time.

By the end, my fingers were hurting, and it was clear I needed more time listening to the tapes and figuring out the little things that the previous guitar player did that made her parts in the songs stand out.

And even then, I knew whatever I did wouldn't save the songs themselves. It was clear the group was far better at playing songs than they were at writing them.

The songs weren't cringeworthy, by any means, but they lacked a spark, a uniqueness that would turn the group into stars.

As the session wrapped up, while I packed my guitar away, Rose crossed the stage and stood over me.

"Okay," she said. "You're fine by me for the weekend. We'll worry about whether it goes any farther once we've finished the shows."

I stood up so I could talk to her on a more even footing. We stood less than a foot apart, and I could smell her, just a whiff of a light perfume, which I didn't expect in the least.

"That's fine with me," I said. "I wasn't expecting this to be a long term thing in the first place."

"Well," she said thrusting a CD into my hand. "If you can't learn the songs by Friday, you won't have to worry about it."

I took the CD, and she walked away.

I couldn't say anything. Somehow, I had just made her mad.

The keyboard player walked up to me while I continued to stand there watching Rose and trying to figure out what I did wrong.

"Hi," the keyboard player said, sticking her hand out. "I'm Carol."

"Hi," I said, even while I tried to peek around her to see what Rose was doing. "I've finally got a name."

Carol laughed.

"That's okay. Nobody ever knows who the keyboard player is."

I couldn't help but chuckle and looked Carol's way. She was pretty enough and was a hell of a player, but compared to the others in the band, she lacked the bit of personality that would make a person stand out.

"So true," I said. "But your playing is incredible."

"Thanks. You don't play guitar so poorly, yourself."

"I'm a bit rusty," I said.

She giggled.

"Rusty? If that's rusty, then I can't wait to see *not* rusty."

"Until four days ago, I hadn't played in a year."

"No one would know," she said.

"I don't believe that."

She lifted one corner of her mouth and scrunched her eyes tight. She put her hand on my shoulder.

"Don't listen to yourself. You're an incredible player. We all know it. You're exactly what we need."

"Rose doesn't think so."

Carol glanced back at Rose, then turned her dark eyes on me.

"Don't believe the words that come out of Rose's mouth. She's so protective of the band, she won't trust anyone. She doesn't even trust Mike."

"I don't even trust him, and he's been my friend forever."

"I'm just trying to make sure you don't let her scare you off. She does this to everybody." And then Carol lowered her voice. "Especially people she likes."

I glanced past Carol at Rose. Rose seemed to be studiously not listening to our conversation while she put away her instrument.

"I don't think she likes me," I said. The idea seemed completely ridiculous. I couldn't even be sure we'd get through the weekend.

"I wouldn't worry about that. There's a reason we cover your songs, and it isn't Adelle. I've been Rose's friend for a long time, and she had a thing for you for years."

Rose slammed her case shut. I guessed she hadn't wanted Carol to spill that information.

It didn't matter, any. It was obvious how Rose felt about me now. She'd be much happier if Mike had brought in some other guitar player.

Just then, Elise bounded up on the stage. It hadn't registered before, but she'd gone right over to Mike after we finished playing.

"I've got an idea," she said, her face all smiles. "Why don't we all go out to Bango's for drinks? Get to know each other?"

"I can't," I said.

"He can't," Rose said, almost simultaneously.

I glanced at her, and she was glaring at me, daring me to contradict her. I also noticed that Mike had sat up a little in his seat. He was watching to see how I would answer.

It didn't matter, though. Drinks were the last thing on my mind at the moment.

I held up the CD.

"I've got work to do," I said. "Maybe tomorrow."

Elise's shoulders drooped a little.

But then she perked right up. "Of course. Tomorrow would be better, anyway."

Tomorrow wouldn't be any better, not for drinks.

"He can't do drinks," Rose said.

Carol rolled her eyes, and Elise opened her mouth to say something, but Rose was looking right at me as she spoke, daring me to contradict her.

"She's right," I said. "But dinner would be awesome."

"Oh Trent," Elise said. "Are you asking us out on a date?"

She ran up to me and embraced me in a tight hug, before pulling back and laughing. I almost wished she hadn't pulled back. It had been awhile since I'd had a hug, and it felt nice. Of course, hooking up with the singer of the band on the first day wouldn't be the smartest move. She probably had a boyfriend, even though she denied it earlier.

"We accept," she said. "There's this awesome Italian place right around the corner from here."

"Tomorrow," I said.

She smiled.

Beyond her, Rose still wore her dour expression.

If Rose did have a crush on me at one time, I didn't think there was any chance she held on to that crush.

Which was probably just as well.

Across the room, Mike was starting to stand.

"Excuse me," I said to Elise and Carol.

"Mike," I called out, turning away from them. "We need to talk."

"Of course," he said. "Meet me in the parking lot. I need a smoke."

I slipped the CD into my guitar case, locked it, and stood up with the case in hand.

"I'll see you all tomorrow," I said. "I had fun."

They all said things, except for Rose, to acknowledge that they had fun, too.

I didn't even register them, though, surprised as I was to find that I had meant what I said.

I did have fun, despite the potential and actual drama that had occurred.

I stepped off the stage, waved, then followed Mike out into the parking lot.

As much fun as I had, and as much as I looked forward to tomorrow, there was something I had to settle with my *friend*.

EIGHT

"So why the hell am I here?" I asked Mike.

We stood underneath an overhang up next to the back wall of the rehearsal studio. While we were inside, the weather had changed, and rain poured down in huge, sloppy drops.

"C'mon, Trent. You know why you're here. They need a guitar player, and you're a perfect fit."

"How am I, in any way, a perfect fit?" I was, of course, ignoring the obvious.

And Mike caught me at it, giving me a sour grimace around his cigarette. Kindly enough, he didn't blow the smoke in my face.

"I mean, besides the obvious."

"You're a guy, they're girls. Elise is hot. You know all the songs. You have experience they could use."

"That's bullshit, Mike. You've got some other reason for hooking me up with them."

Mike took a drag while he decided how he would respond. I knew he was deciding between telling me the whole truth and telling me just enough to get off his back. We'd been friends long enough that I thought he might tell me the whole truth, but he'd done the other often enough that I couldn't trust he was telling me everything, even if he was.

"They're good, aren't they?" Mike asked after he blew his smoke out into the rain.

"That's not what I asked," I said.

"I'm getting to it. Just answer my question."

"Okay, yeah, they are good. Incredible players, to be honest."

"But they can't write for shit, can they?"

I hurriedly glanced around, hoping none of them had followed us out. I didn't want any of them to hear me trash-talking them, not even if it was valid. The parking lot was empty. They were all still inside, probably talking about me like I was talking about them.

"It's not horrible," I said.

"Fine, you're right. It's not horrible. It's just not up to the level of their playing. They need a songwriter. I've tried to get them to work with one, but they refuse every time I suggest it. Rose says they want to do it on their own, or not at all."

I could see that coming out of Rose's mouth. I suspected the band had become her identity.

But this conversation wasn't about Rose.

"So you want me to help them write songs."

"Shit, no. I want you in the band. You felt that first song. I know you did. Elise's voice combined with your music is magical. The two of you together..."

I knew he was seeing dollar signs. I couldn't blame him. It was his job. We might have been long-time friends, but he wouldn't let that come between him and a huge payday. Especially not if he thought he could get me involved in that payday. He would do whatever it took to make it happen.

Which reminded me of something else that had bothered me since Mike mentioned it.

"So, exactly how much are they paying me for this weekend?" I asked.

"I told you," he said. "Three thousand."

He took another drag on his cigarette.

"And how much of that is coming out of your pocket."

He laughed, and it caused him to choke on his smoke.

"Don't do that," he said when he recovered.

I wasn't going to give him the out, though.

"How much, Mike?"

"Twenty-five hundred."

So the band was only paying out five hundred, which was about what I would have expected. Still not bad money for a weekend gig, but certainly not an amount that would have even brought me to the rehearsal.

"Do they know this?"

He shook his head.

"They didn't even know it was going to be you."

I leaned up against the brick wall, set my head against its rough surface.

I took a deep breath, caught a lungful of Mike's smoke. That was just one more thing. I'd have to prepare for the smoke in the club, too.

"I don't know if I can do it, Mike. I haven't written anything in a couple years. Anything good that I wrote happened so long ago."

"It's like a bike," he said. "You could feel that their own songs weren't quite right. As part of the band…"

"I'm not going to be part of the band," I said, making the decision as the words came out of my mouth.

"What?"

"I'll do this weekend, but I'm done after that. Rose won't like me getting in the middle of her shit. It bit me in the ass with Savage Anarchy, and I'm not going to do that again."

Mike dropped the butt of his cigarette to the pavement and ground it under his heel.

"Just think about it, Trent. I know you're feeling like I've tricked you to get you here, and that I'm tricking them, but it's for the better, I swear. You heard it, didn't you? It could be something special."

"No, Mike. I'm not doing this again. I'd just be a great big wedge between them all."

Mike pulled me close and hugged me, patting my back.

"Give it the weekend," he said into my ear. "You'll think differently, then. I swear you will."

He released me, pulled his collar up around his neck, and stepped out into the rain.

He wasn't going to take no for an answer.

But I didn't think he'd have a choice, this time. I couldn't see how there was any chance Rose and I would be able to stand each other over the long haul. She feared I would break up their band, and I couldn't see any way of doing what Mike asked without taking some of the control away from Rose that she held so tight.

It was a disaster waiting to happen.

I took a breath, now free of the taste of smoke, then dove out into the downpour myself.

NINE

I woke up in the middle of the night, hot, sweaty, my heart racing. I could smell Candi in the room.

I reached my arm out, without turning the light on.

There wasn't anyone in bed with me.

I knew she wasn't there with me. She was off, somewhere, looking for the next famous guy with lots of money to take her to parties as often as she could find them.

But I could smell her.

I sat up, still in the dark, and took a deep breath.

It wasn't her I smelled. Just the sheets, the scent of the laundry detergent she used, that I had kept using. Slightly fruity.

It had to go.

I glanced at the clock. Its blue LED numbers blared out the time. Eleven thirty-five. Not even forty minutes after I went to sleep.

I rolled me eyes back into my head, shut them tight, and threw myself back down.

But the smell. The smell was too much.

I got out of bed and stripped the sheets and the blankets off.

I needed the sleep.

After the various stresses of meeting the band, playing Narc Souls songs again, and the conversation with Mike, I had come home and put all my effort into learning the guitar parts for their songs. My fingers were sore, and would hurt tomorrow, but I had the parts down.

And the entire time, I couldn't get the image of Rose's disdain out of my head. For some reason, even though I had no plans to stick around after the weekend, I had to show Rose that I wasn't the loser I had become while with Narcoleptic Souls. I had to show her I was different.

And so I played them again.

And went to bed early, just so I'd be ready.

But the smell.

Candi.

After I had all the sheets off the bed, I lay back down on the bare mattress, my head on a bare pillow.

I could still smell her.

I got up and rolled the sheets into a big ball, then dragged the mess out into the living room and tossed it onto the couch.

I turned to head back into the bedroom, and my eye caught a picture of Candi and I, illuminated by a beam of light from somewhere out in the city.

She was beautiful in the picture, her hair cascading over her left shoulder, her face close to mine with a smile that obscured any hint she was unhappy.

The picture couldn't have been more than six months old.

I couldn't look at it any more.

I knew, just looking at it—that life was dead. Her love was a lie. She used me until I had nothing left to give her, then she moved on.

Such an idiot.

I went over to the picture, picked it up, walked it to the kitchen, opened the door beneath the sink, and tossed the picture in the trash.

A tiny weight, a weight I hadn't know was there, lifted from my shoulders.

Dumping the picture felt good.

She wasn't coming back.

I didn't need to hold on to her shit. I didn't need to hold on to the memory.

Just like it had gone at the rehearsal, earlier, where playing the old songs with new people didn't bring back the memories so much as created new ones.

I'd spent years trying to bury those memories, or forget about them.

And I'd spent months looking at pictures of Candi, looking at the things Candi left behind.

I needed a change.

Mike was right.

He was an asshole, but I couldn't deny any longer that I had to do something different.

A nervous energy built up inside me as I savored the thought.

I couldn't stop myself.

I went through the whole apartment, gathering everything that belonged to Candi, gathering everything that even held a strong memory of her, and dumped it on top of the pile of sheets.

It didn't take very long, fifteen minutes, at most. The pile wasn't as large as I thought it would be, but it was complete.

I had never noticed how few things she had brought into my life. They had all seemed so large, so full of emotion and resonance.

But now, piled on the floor like they were, I realized how inconsequential they were. I finally understood how easy it was for her to leave. She didn't have to take anything with her, because nothing mattered. A suitcase full of clothes, maybe two, and she rolled right out the door.

It was past time for me to get rid of her shit.

I dragged the pile over by the door.

As I was about to turn around to put on something a little more stout than my briefs, I heard a knock at the door.

I put my eye up to the peephole in the door and looked out.

I saw jet black hair and a face that could be either Rose or Adelle. She wore a nondescript leather coat that could have worked for either one of them. The peephole was blurry enough that I could not tell whether the woman outside my door wore a nose ring or not.

I had either a fangirl or a hater at my door, and I didn't know which.

She knocked again while I was looking out.

"Who is it?" I called out.

"It's Rose," she said.

Not who I would have expected.

"Hold on," I said. "I'll be right there."

Why the fuck was Rose outside my door? And at this time of night?

I didn't hear anything from her side of the door, so I dashed into the bedroom, picked the clothes I'd worn earlier in the day off the floor and put them on. Then I hurried back to the door and looked out the peephole again.

She still stood there, patiently waiting.

I opened the door, and stood off to the side to allow her in. She looked at me, then glanced down at the pile of Candi's stuff on the floor.

"Doing some cleaning?" she asked without stepping inside.

"Uh, yeah," I said. "I'm just... just getting rid of some shit." For some reason, I didn't want to tell her whose shit it was.

"Cool," she said. Then she looked at me. "You're shirt's inside out."

As I looked down to find that my shirt *was* inside out, as well as being on backwards, she stepped through the door and past me and stopped next to Candi's pile.

I shut the door, then followed her as she entered the living room.

"This place is kind of bare for a rock star," she said. "I would have expected platinum albums on the wall."

My stomach quivered.

"I like it bare," I said.

"Really?" She pointed a finger up at the wall. "I can see the color difference in the paint where you used to have a whole bunch of things hanging there. I bet that's where you hung them."

I looked, and right where she pointed, there was a slight color variation to the paint on the wall where the plaques had kept the paint behind them from aging in the light.

"They're in storage."

"Ah," she said.

Then she turned away from the wall and looked me over before meeting my eyes with hers.

"You going to fix that shirt?" she asked.

"No reason to," I said. "I'm going to bed right after you leave."

She glanced toward the bedroom door, which stood open. Crap.

She could see that the bed had no sheets on it.

Then she looked back at the pile of Candi's stuff.

"Do you always use your sheets to take your trash out?"

I couldn't answer that, not without talking about Candi, and that was something I was in no hurry to do with Rose.

Besides, something was off, here. Rose seemed nervous, like she had something to say, but was doing anything she could do to keep from saying it.

"Why all the questions?" I asked. "Why are you here?"

She inhaled deeply through her nose, closed her eyes as she did it, then let her breath out slowly before she answered me.

"The others... they..."

I kept still, waiting patiently. This Rose, the woman standing in front of me, was not quite the belligerent, in charge, Rose that I had met earlier in the day.

She took another breath.

"Look," she said. "I'm sorry. I acted like a bitch, this morning, and I shouldn't have. The band is the most important thing in the world to me, and I don't want anything to fuck it up. When Jan got hurt, I thought for a moment it was the end, but..."

Her shoulders were tight, the muscles in her face, tighter. I could almost see her shaking.

I couldn't tell if she wanted to be doing this, or, based on her first words, the others had put her up to it.

In the end, it probably didn't matter. The fact that she had come to my apartment and was apologizing to me was a good indication. Either she wanted to do it, or she thought it was necessary.

Either way, she impressed me.

"I understand," I said. "I've been there. I should apologize, too. There are some subjects that come up, mostly in relation to my last two bands, that are sore subjects, and I can't really control myself or my emotions. I could have reacted better."

"It's not your fault," she said. "Mike told me he deliberately kept you in the dark, as well as us."

"He meant well," I said, "and he was right. If he had told me what the gig was, I would have told him to fuck off."

"And I would have probably told him the same thing," she said, her muscles visibly relaxing a little. There was even a hint of a smile.

For a moment, I thought about telling her what else Mike wanted me to do, but decided against it. I felt, in that moment, that Rose and I might be able to get along, at least for the weekend, and I didn't want to upset that possibility by telling her that Mike thought their own music wasn't good enough.

I didn't want to tell her that I agreed with Mike.

"Well," I said. "At least we have one thing in common."

She did smile at that, the first smile of hers that I had seen. She reached up to push a lock of her hair out of her face.

"It's going to be strange having you in the band, you know," she said. "My sister idolizes you."

"I could tell. You don't have to worry about me. My days of dating fangirls are over."

Rose looked behind her at Candi's things. From this angle, you could just see a picture of Candi and me, the glass cracked from landing awkwardly on the pile when I tossed it on.

"Is that what that is?" Rose asked.

"No," I said.

She tilted her head, as she gave me a questioning look. "You sure?"

I nodded. I felt positive. Fangirls moved in and tried to make you their own. They did everything they could to attach you to them. There wasn't enough in that pile to create or maintain any sort of lasting attachment.

An awkward silence lingered between us, then. I stood uncomfortably, waiting for her to ask something else, and she fidgeted with the hem of the deep maroon blouse she wore under her leather coat.

I had an urge to ask her out for coffee, but I couldn't quite get my mouth to voice the words. The pile of Candi on the floor held me back.

Rose broke the silence.

"Well, that's all I came to say. You've got our songs down?"

"Yeah," I said, "mostly. I still need to rehearse them with the rest of you."

"Of course."

She turned away and moved past Candi's things toward the door.

"I'll see you tomorrow," I said.

"Don't be late," she said over her shoulder as she pulled the door open.

"I won't."

Rose stepped out and shut the door behind her, leaving me alone in the apartment, again.

With each step I took carrying Candi's things toward the dumpster, I kicked myself for not asking Rose out for coffee. There was a moment, and I missed it.

Probably just as well, since I wasn't going to be staying on with the band beyond the weekend.

One thing my cleanout spree had helped me understand—it was time to move on.

And I didn't think going back into the past was the way to do it.

TEN

The feeling at rehearsal the next day was completely different from the first day.

Though Rose wasn't gushing with giddiness at my presence, she also wasn't cold and unwelcoming, either. Businesslike. She accepted that I was part of the band, at least for the moment, and just got on with running the rehearsal.

We started with one of the Narcoleptic Souls songs as a warm up, *Fifteen Ways to Hide From Heaven*, but as soon as that was done, she took us right into rehearsing their own songs.

And it went about like I expected.

I had them down, for the most part. A few memory lapses, but nothing out of the ordinary. We worked those areas over again to make sure I had them down.

Everyone but Rose seemed suitably impressed that I had learned their half dozen songs so quickly. Rose just kept working us until I had them right.

Once we were done with those, we ran through the rest of the set of Narc Souls songs, which I played perfectly, and called it a day after four hours of rehearsing.

It surprised me when Mike didn't show up for the rehearsal. I didn't imagine he would normally show up for their rehearsals, but I thought he would be here for the weekend with me, if only to soothe over any issues.

"I wonder where Mike was," I said, while we were all packing up.

"I told him not to come," Rose said while winding up a guitar cable. "I didn't want the distraction."

I understood. With only a day of rehearsals left, she would have wanted complete focus on the work. I would have, too.

"I get it," I said, and shut the cover of my guitar case. "What's the plan now?"

"Dinner!" Elise said with enthusiasm. "Like we planned. I'm sooo hungry. I didn't eat anything before rehearsal, because I knew we were going to Georgio's."

Rose rolled her eyes.

"I don't know how you can eat at Georgio's all the time," Carol said. "Pasta two, three times a week, yet you never gain weight."

Elise laughed.

"Exercise in the morning, and one meal a day on those days," she said. "It's so good, it's worth it."

"I think she's just naturally gifted," Adelle said from behind us. While Rose and I packed our gear, she sat behind her drums consuming a large, grape sports drink. She was wearing a Narcoleptic Souls shirt that had signatures on it. I didn't see mine, so I don't think she got it while the band was together. I was waiting for her to ask, though. I would have put money down on her having a Sharpie in her purse.

"She's still young," Rose said. "It'll catch up with her."

"You wish," Elise said, running her hands down her sides. "I'll look this way forever. What do you think, Trent?"

She twisted her hips back and forth suggestively, pretending to be something somewhere between a model and a seductress. I wasn't at all comfortable commenting on the topic. Commenting on a woman's eating habits had got me in more trouble on more occasions than I could count.

"Dinner sounds good," I said. "I'm hungry."

Elise and the others laughed.

"Now there's a wise man," Carol said, and everyone laughed again.

Pretty soon, everything we needed for the evening was packed up, and I followed the others out into the parking lot.

I went and put my guitar in the back of my van. After I closed and locked it, I met the girls at the corner of the building.

Elise led us to the end of the block, and then around the corner. About half way to the next light, I saw the restaurant she had mentioned. It had a nice, hand painted sign that said *Georgio's Pizza & Pasta*. It was a hole in the wall kind of place, from what I could see. I didn't imagine there were more than a dozen tables inside. Outside, it had a small dining area, fenced off with wrought iron. Inside the area stood three tables protected by an awning. It was too damned cold to eat outside. The tables were empty, waiting for an intrepid diner to sit down.

When we stepped inside the place, I discovered that my assessment of the place from the outside was correct.

There couldn't have been more than ten tables, carefully separated by privacy walls. The lights were kept at a nice level for comfortable dining. The decor was about what you'd expect from an Italian restaurant: wine bottles everywhere, paintings of grapes, bread, and pasta.

A family of four sat at one table. Other than that, the place was empty. Not too surprising at four in the afternoon.

We weren't waiting more than two minutes to be seated when a man, perhaps in his mid twenties, hair cut short, gleaming eyes, and a smile that exposed teeth that had no business being so white, approached us.

"Elise, glad to see you again."

"Hey, Benny," she said.

"Everyone else, too," he said, nodding in our direction. "Who's the new guy?"

"He's Jan's replacement," Elise said. She grew a mischievous look. "You're going to love seeing him play. He seems to have a special attachment to the Souls' music. You going to be there tomorrow?"

Benny looked at me, studying for a moment.

"A special connection?" He continued to study me for another minute before turning back to Elise. "Well, I guess that means I'll have to be there. You want your usual table?"

"Of course," she said.

Benny grabbed a stack of menus from the top of a small table to our right, then turned toward the seating area of the restaurant.

"This way, then."

We followed him to the table, a big round booth in the corner with the three-quarter circular bench where everyone had to slide in.

I ended up in the middle between Carol and Adelle. Elise and Rose were on the ends, if that's what you would call them. There was more than enough room for all of us, but Adelle sat a little closer than strictly necessary.

It was the first fangirl move of hers since she first walked into the rehearsal room the previous day.

I wondered what Rose might think of her sister's behavior, but when I glanced her way, she was already looking through the menu.

"You'll love this place," Adelle said. "I like the Pollo con Fresca."

I hadn't a clue what that even was.

I saw movement out of the corner of my left eye, and noticed that Rose had dipped her menu down slightly so that she could peer over the edge of it. As soon as she saw me looking, she lifted the menu back up.

"They've got good pizzas, too," Carol said.

I wondered if I would get a recommendation from each of them.

"Shall we start with drinks?" Benny asked.

Elise started off, asking for a chardonnay. Adelle asked for a dark ale that I've never heard of.

"I'll have water," I said.

I heard Adelle whisper, "Oh, yeah." And then she said louder, "Can I change mine? I'd like water, instead."

Another fangirl move.

"You don't need to watch what you drink on my account," I said.

"No, no," she said, putting her hand on my wrist. "It's just when you said it, it sounded good."

"I'll have a lime soda," Carol said.

I pulled my wrist out from under Adelle's hand and lifted up my menu, while glancing at Rose. She was still hiding behind her menu.

"And you, Rose?" Benny asked.

"Huh?" She looked startled, dropped her menu flat to the table as her head jerked toward the sound of Benny's voice. "Oh, yeah. An Amalfi Lemonade."

"What's that?" I asked.

Benny turned to me.

"Blackberry vodka, lemonade, and soda with a black raspberry liqueur. Would you like to try one?"

"Ah, no thanks," I said, even though I would have loved to try one. The problem being, if I had tried one, I might try another, and another. Best just to stay away.

I found it interesting that Rose had ordered alcohol, considering what she thought of my past. Of anyone, I would have thought she would have been the one to push the others to abstain. I glanced at her, but she wasn't even looking at me. She had buried herself back in the menu.

For a moment, I thought she might be testing me, but then Adelle shifted next to me, and I wondered if maybe Rose was trying to prove something to her sister.

And thinking about that reminded me of all the shit I went through with Savage Anarchy. I closed my eyes for a moment while I tried to suppress those memories, but I couldn't keep them from surfacing.

ELEVEN

People jostled each other as they walked by, packed into the club so tight that the only way through the mass was to push through whatever space you could find. It always amazed me how few fights broke out among the crowd in a place like this, especially when it was a Savage Anarchy crowd.

You wouldn't know it to look at them, but Savage Anarchy crowds were made up of some of the nicest people I had ever met. Especially the ones that made it to the club gigs.

The arena shows pulled the losers from the rest of humanity, but the club shows were filled with true fans, the people I could relate to.

Which was more than I could say for the other members of the band.

I could hardly relate to them at all.

And they weren't at all interested in making it easy on me. They mostly thought that not drinking was just a matter of not drinking. I don't think they realized it was a matter of life and death.

I turned away from my peek at the audience through the curtain to find Johnny B. standing there behind me. His hair, black and full of who knows what, stood out at all angles. He had a glass in his hand, full of whiskey. The smell of it was strong enough, I knew he hadn't cut it with anything.

"What're you doing, Trent? Checkin' the crowd?"

"Yeah," I said.

"You think it'll be a good night?"

Johnny lifted the glass to his lips and drank. Half of it disappeared like that.

Another one of those nights.

I knew we'd be lucky if the show didn't end in a fight.

"I hope so," I said. I wasn't thinking about the crowd, though.

"You want a drink?" he asked, holding his up to me.

I shook my head.

"Of course not. You never drink, damned straight arrow. Steve wants to start with *Mirror Dark*. I think it's bullshit. What do you think?"

"I'm fine with it," I said.

Johnny's eyes narrowed.

Then his fist flashed out like a shot and caught the left side of my jaw, knocking me backward, out through the curtain and into the walkway between the dressing room entrance and the stage.

The roar of a thousand voices cheering assaulted my ears. It lasted until they realized something wasn't quite right.

I stood for a second, feeling my jaw, trying to keep my anger below boiling.

It was Johnny being Johnny, and he was half-drunk, if not completely drunk, to boot.

But I couldn't keep the anger down any longer.

I'd stayed so long because it was a gig and it made money.

But money wasn't enough for me to put up with this asshole, or any of them, really.

Johnny peeked his head out beyond the curtain to see the result of his punch.

My anger boiled up. All I could see was him taunting me every day with his drinking, pushing my buttons because I was the one person in the band everyone knew. They'd brought me in because of my fame, and it worked. Their fan base grew, just as they'd wanted.

But Johnny couldn't take it. And he was only getting worse.

I prepped myself to rush him.

I wanted to take his head off.

I was sick and tired of the bullshit.

I remembered, somehow, things my therapist said. He taunted me about her, too.

I took a deep breath, closed my eyes for half a second, even though I knew Johnny was standing there watching, even though I knew he could pounce on me.

I let the breath out.

And then I turned my back on Johnny and hopped the rope that separated us from the crowd.

I pushed my way through the throng.

People made space as they realized who I was.

They patted me on the back, said "I love you, man!"

But it wasn't enough to keep me from leaving.

TWELVE

"What are you thinking about?"

Adelle's voice brought me out of the memory.

"What? Oh, nothing."

"It wasn't nothing," she said.

I looked her way. She had the same dark eyes as Rose, the same hair. At least, on the surface, she liked me more. She was willing to overlook the past in a way that I didn't think Rose would.

But I couldn't really ignore the past, or overlook it, no matter how much I wanted to. If I did that, I'd only end up right back where I was—drinking my first meal of the day, and keeping the buzz going until I went to bed at night.

And the altercations with Johnny B. were indicative of what could happen when I step on someone's toes and just ignore that I did so. He couldn't handle having someone in the band that was more famous than him, and I had ignored the signs until it all blew up.

I wasn't going to make that mistake again, either.

"It was nothing I want to talk about," I said.

"Oh."

I don't know what she heard in my voice, but it seemed for a moment that her fangirl enthusiasm faded just a little. Maybe, for the first time, she saw a real person in me. I don't know. I would have hoped she saw that on the first day.

Just then, Benny returned with the drinks and handed them out.

"Can I take your orders?" he asked.

The others nodded, but I realized I hadn't even looked at my menu. I'd been off in the old world I wanted to put behind me, but couldn't.

Benny began with Elise, while I quickly opened my menu and started reading through it. I hoped I could find a dish that wasn't too pasta heavy—in an Italian restaurant. Right.

"You want your usual, Elise?" Benny asked.

"Of course," she said.

I didn't have to see the smile to know she smiled. I could hear it in her voice.

Looking down the menu, I found pastas, salads (I'm not much of a salad eater), and more pastas.

Adelle chose the Pollo con Fresco, which didn't surprise me, as she had suggested it earlier.

"Sir?" Benny asked.

I chuckled inside. "Sir" was my father. Not me. It always seemed odd having it directed at me. Even with my fame, the expensive hotels we had stayed in, I still hadn't really quite got over the feeling that anyone calling me sir was talking to someone else.

"I'm still looking," I said. "Get the others."

Which is what he should have done, anyway. Ladies first, right?

There were a bunch of chicken dishes, but they were all served with pasta, too. I wasn't in the mood for pizza, either. Too much bread.

Basically, I was left with two options. Steak, which always seemed wrong in an Italian restaurant, and a salmon dish with sauteed veggies and garlic mashed potatoes.

Carla ordered a chicken pesto pizza.

When Rose ordered, my ears perked up.

"I'll have the Salmon Picatta," she said.

Exactly what I had decided to order.

And then the thoughts started in. I'd have to order something different so that she wouldn't think I was ordering the salmon to please her. No. I should order the salmon, because I wanted to please her. But I shouldn't. Adelle might take it wrong. And Elise? Carol? What would they think? There wasn't anything else on the menu.

Fuck!

Why did I care, anyway? Rose wouldn't. It wasn't as if I was interested in her.

"I'll have the Salmon Picatta, too," I said before Benny could even ask me the question again.

Rose looked at me, but her expression didn't betray any of the thoughts going on in her head.

"That's a good choice," Benny said. He put his pad in his pocket, and walked away.

Holy hell.

Rose's look didn't last but more than a second or two, however long that seemed to me.

"Let's talk about tomorrow," she said.

Tomorrow. Right. The show.

"First, rehearsal is early. Ten in the morning. We haven't worked at all with Trent on the choreography, and he'll have to get that down."

"Wait, what?" I asked. "Choreography?"

"Yeah," Elise said. "We've got moves laid out for every song. They're not hard, but you will need to be able to get your knee up to your nose."

"What the hell?"

"Mike didn't tell you?" Rose asked.

"No. He didn't tell me anything."

"Well, we'll just have to trust he knows how flexible you are. We can't have you wearing Jan's outfit without you doing the moves."

I leaned my head back, rolled my eyes, and started to chuckle. They were busting me.

"Why are you laughing?" Adelle asked.

"You guy's are just fucking with me," I said.

"No we're not," Carol said, her voice a pretty decent imitation of sincerity. "We're an all girl band. You've got to play the part."

"But I'm not..."

They all broke out laughing.

"Of course you're not," Elise said. "You'd make an ugly girl. You'll just have to find something in your closet and try to look like you belong."

"And the choreography?"

"A pile of lies," Rose said. "But the look on your face was priceless. We might just have to think about adding some choreography to the act, just to see you dance."

"I'm not dancing," I said.

"No?"

"No."

Rose's phone rang, and she answered it.

"Hey."

She gave no indication of who it was.

"We're all at Georgio's."

A half second went by.

"Yeah, he's here, too."

Her eyebrows lifted as if she had just received some interesting news.

"Really? What is it?"

A couple seconds passed.

"Hurry, then. We'll be here."

Then she hung up.

"Who was that," I asked.

"Mike. He says he's got some good news."

"What is it," Elise asked.

But I already knew Mike was saving it for the in-person reveal. It was the same reason he showed up at the rehearsal the day before, but not the one we just finished.

"He wouldn't say," Rose said. "He's coming down here to share it with us."

And whatever it was, it was something Mike wanted me to hear.

I started looking for Benny, hoping he would hurry with the food. If I could finish before Mike arrived...

I wasn't sure I wanted to hear what Mike had to say.

THIRTEEN

Mike arrived a few minutes later, his long hair pulled back into a pony tail. He had a huge grin on his face— the kind you might wear if you just made a million bucks.

He found our table, walked straight over and squeezed in next to Elise, forcing the rest of us to scoot over, too.

"How was rehearsal, today?" he asked.

"Productive," Rose said. "We'll be ready for the show."

"Good." Mike glanced at me. "I told you he'd work out."

Just then Benny came over.

"Can I get you anything?" he asked.

"No thanks. I won't be staying. I've just got to give these girls some good news, and then I'll be going."

"Sure thing," Benny said. "I'll be around if you change your mind."

And then Benny left the table, but he didn't go far. He busied himself at a nearby table, wiping it down, rearranging the condiments and other table toppers. That wasn't what he was really doing, though. He was listening. He knew the girls, and probably knew Mike, or at least, knew who he was.

"So what's the news, Mike?" Rose asked.

"Both shows are sold out," he said.

"Sold out?" Elise asked.

"How did that happen?" Carol asked immediately after. "We've never sold out that place before."

"Not even close," said Adelle.

"Someone discovered that Trent was joining you for the gigs, and it got out on the radio this morning."

"Discovered?" Rose asked with a detectable note of anger in her voice. "How did anyone discover it? You didn't even tell us until yesterday."

But I knew how. Mike had it planned all along.

I didn't know whether to be angry at him, or myself. I should have expected something like this. Mike wasn't anything if he wasn't a promoter. Expecting Mike to set me up with a band, and then *not* whisper things in the ears of people who care about this kind of shit was like expecting ice to not melt in the summer sun.

"You leaked it," I said.

"Three different radio stations," he said with a smile on his face. He was proud of what he'd done.

I caught sight of Benny. Now, he stood just off to the side, no longer pretending to straighten out the tables. He was listening intently. If he knew who I was, he didn't show it. But he was guaranteed to head straight into the back, hop on his phone, and find out.

"I can't believe you did that, Mike," Rose said. "Not without asking us, first. What if he hadn't worked out?"

"I knew he would work out. I could hear it yesterday. Whether it goes longer than just this weekend, well, that's up to you, but I knew he'd be here for the weekend, and we needed to capitalize on it."

"Get out, Mike," Rose said while sitting utterly still. "I don't want to see you right now."

"What's wrong?"

"You should have warned us. You should have *asked* us, before you turned this weekend into a sideshow."

The grin fell away from Mike's face.

"I don't understand. I thought you'd be excited that the shows sold out. My job is to get shows for you, get deals for you, and get you as much money as possible."

"Your job is to help the band get to where we want to go. You've promoted Trent over the band. We didn't sell those shows out." She pointed a finger at me. "He did."

And she was right.

What Mike had done crossed the line. Again. But I understood why he did it. He's paying me to do this gig, and he'll take less of a hit with the shows sold out. Even if he promotes me, the band gets exposure to people who wouldn't normally have heard of them. Those people might come to future shows.

"Does it really matter?" Adelle asked. "Those people will see us, even if they're coming to see him. We play his music, after all."

"It totally matters," Rose said. "You don't get it. You never do. It's our own songs that will take us where we want to be. Playing Narc Souls songs bring in money, but we can't play them forever. These people will come expecting to see a reinvented Narc Souls, and that's not who we want to be, is it?"

And just like that, Mike had created a crisis within the band, with me at the center of it.

As if Rose needed yet another reason to not want me in the band. I refused to examine my feelings about that. I was still only going to be in the band for the next two days.

"Of course it's not who we want to be," Elise said. Her face, for the first time in the two days I'd known her, had a serious look on it. "But it's who we are, right now, isn't it?"

"You know why we're doing this. We all like the music, it pays well, and we need the money," Rose said. "It's not who we are."

Mike sat back against the seat rest, and watched while the argument started. I caught him glancing over at me once or twice while the discussion around us grew more heated. I got the distinct impression that he'd planned for this to happen.

I thought about the songwriting discussion Mike and I had the day before.

And for a moment, I saw what he saw.

The girls had talent. They were musically gifted, and they were slogging away playing someone else's songs. They needed a push, and he intended for me to be that push.

I was angry at Mike. I did not want to be in the spotlight at all, not with the shit I was dealing with. I just wanted to play the weekend, collect my cash, and...

I stopped.

The argument between Elise and Rose had expanded to encompass all four of the girls, but I didn't actually hear any of it.

I was stuck on the idea that I had no idea what I would do after the weekend.

Candi was gone, and I had completely removed every trace of her from my apartment.

I didn't have a band, or a job, beyond the weekend.

I knew I'd take the three thousand, pay my rent and food and other bills for another month.

And then what?

I looked at Mike again, this time, straight at him, until he noticed me looking.

He wasn't just pushing them.

"You bastard," I said.

It happened to fall into a silence that had just opened up as the girls thought about whatever their next salvo might be.

Everyone turned and looked at me.

Mike smiled.

"What's your point?" he asked.

"There are better ways to get what you want than this," I said.

"What are you talking about?" Elise asked.

I didn't look away from Mike. He was my friend, and I knew he manipulated people for his own ends. And I'd forgotten it.

"He planned this argument," I said. "He picked me as Jan's replacement because he knew he could do exactly this. He wanted you to have exactly this discussion, because he knew it would force you to think about your future."

Mike nodded, and the girls turned to look at him.

"And I don't know how I didn't see it, or remember, but he pulled almost this same kind of stunt to get me in with Savage Anarchy."

And as I said it, the memory came flooding back. They were a nothing band, struggling to make money on the club circuit. They couldn't write songs for shit.

Mike introduced them to me, suggested I play along with them, and I was still just trying to stay sober in that moment. I needed an anchor, and I took it.

But it was quickly clear that Johnny B. didn't want me in the band. He thought I was there to take his place as the leader. However, through tricks and innuendo and money, Mike was able to get the rest of the band to convince Johnny that I should be in the band.

It wasn't exactly the same thing, here, though.

But it wasn't all that different.

And I hadn't seen it, because of Candi.

Mike was there, again, to take advantage of my weaknesses.

"This is completely different," Mike said, "and you know it."

"What are you talking about, Trent?" Rose asked.

"This is not different, Mike. Sure, last time, I asked you to find me a gig, and this time, you came to me. Last time, the tricks were different, because you only had to convince Johnny, but you still set things up to impress him. You never told him why you chose to introduce me to them."

"He knew exactly why," Mike said. His eyes twitched in his head. He was begging me not to reveal why he wanted me in this band with these girls.

"He didn't. You booked us shows with bigger acts using my name to get us in. You publicized the shit out of me being in the band. At the time, I didn't mind. I was used to it. I expected big shows. It might as well have been Trent Richards and Savage Anarchy, the way you promoted it."

"That's bullshit. You wanted all of that. You begged me to get you bigger shows. I did what you wanted. And I didn't do it all the time."

"No. After awhile, you didn't have to. But that doesn't matter, now. The point is that you're hoping to use me as a way to push this band big, probably before they're ready. And it'll end up the same way, though I hope Rose will refrain from punching me in the face like Johnny B. did."

The last little joke failed to lighten the mood.

The whole table was silent, everyone focused on me.

"It's a shame you feel that way, Trent," Mike said. "You're only filling in for the weekend, so you've said. Maybe you'll change your mind, but can you fault me for wanting to try to fill the place while you're there?"

At that moment, Benny arrived with our meals. He handed them out quickly, without saying anything.

He may have been listening in on our conversation, but he knew how to be circumspect. I appreciated that.

When he finished, he asked us if we needed anything else.

The mood at the table was so tense, none of us but Elise uttered a word.

All she said was, "No thank you."

And the entire time Benny was busy at our table, I tried to figure out how to answer Mike's question.

I couldn't really fault him for wanting to make as much money on the deal as he could. I'm sure he was hoping to make enough to cover what he had said he would pay me.

But the way he was doing it had my guts twisted in knots.

Savage Anarchy was what it was. We all made out on the deal. They got big like they wanted, and I got to continue playing rock star, at least until I got tired of the bullshit of dealing with Johnny.

But this was different.

I actually liked these girls. Even Rose was growing on me, and I think she was warming up to me, too.

The band was important to them in a way my other bands never had been important to me. Maybe it was because they were women. Maybe it was because they were all good friends. I hadn't been with them long enough to be able to put a finger on it. Two days was not enough time.

I didn't think it was right for Mike to risk that, and for that, I could fault him.

"Alright, Mike," I said. "I can't fault you for wanting to make money. But Rose is right. By promoting my presence for this gig, you've gone for the money instead of doing right by the band and what they want."

"It's a business, Trent. They need more people to see them. I've just guaranteed they're going to be seen by three times as many people as would have seen them without the promotion."

I could smell the salmon in front of me, and it made my mouth water, but my stomach roiled. I needed to calm down. I needed Mike to go.

"They're not coming to see the band, though. They're coming to see a version of Narcoleptic Souls. Those people will forget the band within a week. They might not even remember the name the next day. You're not doing them any favors."

Mike stood up.

"I've got to run," Mike said. "But Trent, some of them will remember, and that will be more than before. If you stayed beyond the weekend, would it hurt them at all? Would it even matter?"

My anger roared up inside me. I felt the urge to crash my fist through his jaw. I would have stood up and tried if I wasn't locked in behind the table.

"Don't you even try to lay this on me," I said. "Go to your fucking meeting. Go make more money. It's all you care about, isn't it?"

Mike leaned over the table and stared right at me.

"Don't think about fucking with me, Trent. I can see to it that whatever bands you join will never make it out of the garage. This business is all about money. Art for art's sake is fine, but it's a pipe dream once you have to feed yourself off of it.

"You know how Rose felt about you when she first walked in? I can make that happen everywhere you go. No one will want to work with you."

"I'd sue you," I said.

How the fuck did the conversation go so wrong?

"With what money? You're broke. Do the gig. I'll see you after, when you've come to your senses."

He pushed himself back up, turned, and left.

Not a one of us said a word.

I looked down at my salmon.

I wasn't hungry anymore.

I just wanted to throw up.

I needed some fresh air.

I slid down beneath the table, and as inelegant as the move was, I didn't care. I couldn't get my mouth open to ask the girls to let me out.

I ran outside, let the door shut behind me, and took a deep breath.

The air felt cold in my lungs, and it calmed the fire, just a little bit. My stomach and my chest were still tight.

I took more breaths, each one calming, but not nearly enough.

Mike had always looked out for me, or so I thought. He got me gigs, got me alcohol, got me women. He did whatever I asked.

And it had taken me until just that moment, just that argument, for me to realize that he and I were never really friends. I was a well paid, well pampered, cog in his machine. I was just another pawn on the board that he could move around to make him money.

The door behind me opened, announcing it did so with the sound of little bell chimes. I didn't turn to see who it was. I suspected Adelle or Elise had come out to see how I was doing, but I didn't really want to talk to them just then.

"You want to talk about it?" Rose asked.

She was the last person I had expected to come out.

I surprised myself by saying, "Yes."

FOURTEEN

I gave Rose money to cover my bill for the salmon I wasn't going to eat, and she went inside and paid for it while I waited just outside the door.

When she came back out, she looked at me with a softness in her eyes that I hadn't seen, yet.

"Why don't we walk," she said.

"Sure," I said.

We didn't say anything for a few minutes as we walked down the street. We walked slowly. I couldn't stop thinking about what I'd just realized about Mike, but I didn't know how to put it into words.

We came to a crosswalk, waited for the light, and then crossed before either of us spoke a word.

The part of town we were in had a lot of unique shops, antiques, curiosities, an old record shop that sold records and not CDs.

I didn't see any of them as we walked, though.

I only saw Mike, standing over the table, threatening my livelihood.

"I met him just as Narcoleptic Souls was getting off the ground," I said. "We were still in our garage, playing local shows to a dozen people in the diviest of bars. He came to one of the shows, then approached me afterward and said he'd like to manage us.

"And then he handed me a card. He wasn't just some joker who thought it would be cool to be a manager. He had an actual business. I couldn't believe our luck."

"That sounds familiar," Rose said.

"Yeah, I discovered later that he likes to go to all the local bars and see the bands play, especially when they don't draw anyone. He's looking for the act that no one else has seen that he can turn into mega-stars.

"And he did it with us. He did it with Savage Anarchy, too. He pushed us to rehearse more, got us into bigger venues and onto larger bills. The whole thing just ballooned. In some ways, I miss those days. Mike and I were as close as can be.

"At least, I thought we were."

"Why aren't you, now?" Rose asked.

We came to another crosswalk, and had to stop for the light to change.

I looked down at her, though with her heels, we were only a couple inches different in height. She had her eyes riveted on me, paying attention in a way that was both scary and flattering.

"I'm not sure we ever were," I said. "I'm beginning to think that he doesn't have any real friends. That he's just playing a game to get the people he works with to do what he wants. You heard him. He's really just in it for the money, and probably the prestige it gets him. The power."

Rose nodded.

The pixelated person hanging off the light pole on the other side of the street turned from red to green.

"I did see that," she said. "I've actually known since I met him. I did my homework before we signed with him."

"Smart, though if you knew what he was, why did you sign?" I asked.

Pixelated person started flashing.

"He turned Narcoleptic Souls and Savage Anarchy into household names. Other bands, too. He has a great track record. I figured we could manage him, if we were careful."

Pixelated person turned red without us crossing.

"I never saw something like this happening, though," Rose said.

"You never saw Jan leaving the band. Shit happens."

"I never saw you coming into the band," she said.

"He manipulated me," I said.

"Manipulated you?"

I took a deep breath. I was pissed enough at Mike that I decided I was going to spill everything to Rose. She deserved to know it. She wanted to be where I had been, and she was right that Mike knew how to get her there, but she didn't know how he would do it.

I looked at the various storefronts to see if I could find a place for us to sit.

"Over there," I said, pointing. "That little coffee shop. Let's go sit down, and I'll tell you."

"Okay," she said.

When pixelated person turned green again, we crossed, then sat down at one of the outside tables. It was chilly, and there was a slight breeze, but I didn't want to go inside. I didn't really want coffee, just a place to sit.

She sat across from me, and I looked into her eyes as she spoke.

"Mike's paying me three thousand for the gig this weekend."

Rose blinked.

"Three thousand? That's more than our whole take, most weekends. It makes sense why he would want to fill the place."

"Yeah, I know. He made me think you all were an established band already, and that you'd fill the place. I thought I was just coming in to be a nobody guitar player for a band that needed help for a weekend."

"What you're saying is that he intended to do this all along."

"Probably," I said while picking at the iron weave of the table with my fingers. "He might have thought of advertising the shows after he realized I was serious about not staying on with the band after the weekend."

"Which probably ensures that you won't stay on," she said. Somehow, she sounded a bit disappointed.

"You sound like you were thinking of having me stay."

She smiled a thin smile.

"I've thought about it. The way you play, even using Jan's equipment, the sound of the band seems so much fuller. I can feel your playing in a way that I can't describe. I was going to wait and see what happened with the shows before I said anything, but after you defended my position to Mike back there, I don't think I need to wait any longer."

"Well, there's more you should hear, first, before you go making any decisions."

My heart beat faster as I realized I was going to tell her. "What is it?" she asked.

I took a deep breath, then spit out the words as fast as I could.

"Mike wanted me in the band, because he thinks your songwriting skills are weak."

Her response surprised me.

"You agree with him, don't you?"

I wasn't about to lie to her, but I didn't want to agree. I've never liked passing judgment on other people's work.

She waited while I said nothing, while I tried to figure out how to say it without sounding like an asshole to my ears.

"Your silence is enough," she said.

She sat back in her chair, looked out into the street and watched the cars go by. I couldn't tell what she was thinking. I hadn't known her long enough.

I was about to open my mouth and say something, when she sighed, turned back to me, then pushed herself out of her chair.

"Okay, I get it." Her voice was a lot colder than it was just a minute ago. "I understand, and it makes perfect sense. I'll see you tomorrow. Get to the rehearsal room early. We have to move all our gear to the club, and then we'll have a last rehearsal there."

I stood up, too.

"But..."

"No, don't say anything," she said. "You don't need to apologize for thinking the way you do. I just need to think. Thanks for letting me know."

And then she walked past me, back the way we came, her arms locked across her chest.

I had thought while we walked that maybe we were growing closer, coming to an understanding. I had thought we were of like mind.

And now, I had ruined it.

But it was probably for the best. She would have had to learn what Mike thought at some point. And if I had stayed, she would have learned what I thought, too.

Two more days.

I'd do the shows, and then she wouldn't have to deal with me again.

Mike, on the other hand, I was glad she knew what he thought. It may hurt for a little while, but at least they wouldn't get trapped into his ideas for the band. At least they wouldn't end up like Narc Souls or Savage Anarchy.

And thinking that made me smile, even as I watched Rose cross the street in the distance.

She may hate me, but I did her some good.

If only I had someone to celebrate that success with.

FIFTEEN

I can always count on Jessica to know when to call. Half-way home, my phone started ringing in my pocket. I fumbled it out while driving down the freeway, and managed to get it answered and set to speakerphone without crashing or disconnecting the call.

"Trent! Why haven't you called me?"

Jessica and I have been friends forever, even before Narc Souls. We talk maybe once or twice a year, now, and always end with the sentiment that we should talk more often, but up until this past year, my life had been so hectic with always being on the road that it was almost impossible. She had a life, too, with being a somewhat successful author of fiction for twenty-something women—lots of steamy sex and hot guys and figuring out how to be an adult. Not my type of thing.

"I've been busy."

"Busy? Last I heard, you quit Savage Anarchy and weren't doing much at all."

"If you were in town, I'd tell you all about it, but right now, I'm on the road, heading home from rehearsal."

"Oh, good! Meet me at the University Bookstore. I'm doing a reading there tonight. We can go for drinks after, and you can fill me in on all the details."

What were the chances?

"You know I don't drink," I said.

"I know. I'll drink. You talk. Like old times."

I didn't really want to go listen to her read, and I certainly wasn't interested in watching her drink, but we hadn't seen each other in a long time, and I had just been moaning to myself about needing someone to talk to, to celebrate with.

And maybe she'd have some ideas on how to deal with the situation.

"Alright, fine. What time?"

"The reading starts at seven thirty."

"I'll be there at eight," I said.

She laughed.

"The sex still too much for you?"

"Always."

"Don't be late," she said. "I've got to catch a flight out tomorrow morning, so I can't stay up all night."

"Gotcha. I'll be prompt."

"See you soon," she said. "This'll be fun."

Then she hung up, and I continued to drive home.

SIXTEEN

I arrived at the bookstore at two-minutes 'til eight.

When I walked through the doors, I could see Jessica in the center of the store, sitting at a table, a line of women waiting with books in their arms to have her sign them. There were a few men, too, but each of them was attached to one of the women in line, and none of them looked particularly interested in being there.

I couldn't blame them.

If I'd had to sit through the reading, I'd want to be somewhere else, too.

Fortunately, Jessica never minded that I didn't want to sit through them—at least, not after I sat through the first one.

I skirted the line and went around a few shelves until I could approach Jessica from the other side.

Jessica looked as good as ever, full-bodied blond hair cut short at the shoulders, sharp cheek lines and sparkling eyes that accentuated the joy on her face and drew attention away from her beak of a nose. She was in her element, and it showed.

She glanced up, saw me, and waived me over.

When I came up to the table, she said, "Excuse me," to the woman whose book she was signing, stood up and gave me a hug.

"It's good to see you," she said.

"Good to see you, too."

"I've got another half hour, or so," she said. "Pull up a chair. Maybe one of the guys in line will want you to sign something."

I laughed, only because it was true, then looked around for a chair while Jessica sat back down and finished signing the woman's book. My laugh surprised me, because I wasn't in any mood to sign anything for anyone.

The way Jessica worked her signings, we didn't have a lot of time to talk. She paid attention to every single person that came through the line, asking who they wanted it signed to, engaging in chit-chat with them for a minute or so while she pondered appropriate things to write on the title page of every number one fan.

"How's James," I asked, at one point.

James was an old buddy of mine that Jessica had married. Jessica and I were closer than James and I were, but talking about him was a safe topic in the public eye. Especially since I didn't want any more news about what was happening with me to get out.

"He's good," she said. "He's at home with the kids, probably playing games after the kids go to bed. He's taken over most of the business side of things, now. It was cheaper than hiring an assistant."

I laughed. I had a hard time imagining James sitting at home taking care of kids. He'd been as rough and tumble a rocker as I knew, back then. Partied every night, slept until it was time for a show.

"You need to bring him with you one of these times," I said.

"Thank you for coming," she said to one of her fans. "I hope you enjoy the book."

The next fan stepped up to the table. She had dreadlocks in her red hair, a ring through her nose, and looked as thin as a sapling.

"Who am I signing for?" Jessica asked.

"Cherise," she said. "I've been a fan of yours since your first book."

"I love hearing that," Jessica said.

Then she got to signing, and Cherise (I assumed that was her name) looked over at me.

"I'll be at your show tomorrow," she said. "I've been waiting to see what you do next. Your music is amazing."

"Uh, thanks," I said. "It's not my band, though. I'm just filling in."

"Oh, that's a shame. I've been looking forward to something new from you ever since they railroaded you out of Savage Anarchy."

The punch.

Someone had caught it on camera, and the entertainment news had picked it up. Johnny B. spun it as him kicking me out of the band, saying that I was disruptive and a bad influence.

Which was bullshit.

I hadn't bothered to fight it, though. The band was his, and I didn't want any part of it, or the drama, anymore.

And so everyone bought Johnny B's version of the story.

But every once in awhile, I ran into a fan that didn't believe the spin.

"I don't know what's going to happen, honestly," I said. "I took some time off to clear my head. This gig this weekend is just me helping out some friends. I don't know how the radio picked up on it."

That last was a lie, but I wasn't about to expose a rift between me and Mike to a fan.

Jessica handed the book back to Cherise, and smiled.

"Thanks for coming and giving him someone to talk to," she said, laughing. "I think he was getting bored talking to me."

Cherise laughed.

Then she handed the book to me.

"Would you mind signing it? I didn't think I'd ever see my favorite author and my favorite musician sitting next to each other."

I took the book, and grabbed a pen out of a jar of them that the bookstore had set up for Jessica.

I thought about being all rock and roll and signing the cover, but decided, instead, that if she liked seeing the two of us together, she would probably enjoy seeing our names together, too. I turned to the page where Jessica had signed, and beneath her signature, I wrote, 'Thanks for being cool,' and signed my name.

I handed it back to her.

She opened the book up, looked at it, then hugged it to her chest.

"Thank you so much," she said. "This was so awesome. I'll see you tomorrow night."

Then she turned and walked away, and the next Jessica fan approached the table.

"So, I guess you've got some female fans, too," Jessica said while she waited for the woman to hand her a book to sign.

"What? I've got fans of both sexes," I said. "I'm an equal opportunity rock star, baby."

Jessica asked the woman who she was signing for before she replied to me.

"I've seen the people that go to your shows. It's eighty-five percent men."

"It's a shame, then, that you're leaving tomorrow morning," I said. "You'd probably enjoy the show."

"You know I would. I've always liked your work."

"The band is all women."

"All women?" she asked. "I didn't realize you had an operation."

"Well, it's all women, except for me."

"Ah. You should learn to be more specific."

"You should learn not to analyze the English of a guitar god."

Jessica handed the now signed book back to the woman, who left and made room for the next one.

"Guitar god," she said. "That's funny. You know I'd go tomorrow, if I could, but the publisher set up this itinerary, and they're paying for the whole deal. I can't really change my plans."

"I didn't think they were doing that stuff, anymore," I said.

"They do it for me," she said while signing another book. "I don't know how much effect it has on sales, and I hate the travel, but I enjoy seeing my fans."

I used to enjoy seeing my fans, too.

Like Cherise.

The ones from the Narc Souls days.

Not the fans of Savage Anarchy.

"How much longer will we be seeing your fans?" I asked.

She looked out over the line, and glanced at her watch. The line was shorter, but still not short.

"Another twenty minutes, or so."

"Good," I said. "I've got some other news I want to talk to you about that I can't really share in public."

"Oh?" she asked without ever taking her eyes off the book she was signing.

"Yeah. But not here."

"I'll go as fast as I can, then, Mr. Guitar God."

She didn't bother picking up her pace, though.

Every fan got just as much attention as she'd given to every other fan, and I had to admire her stamina and her ability to relate with them.

I even signed a couple more items, one for one of the guys in line, and another book for a woman that happened to be a fan of us both, just like Cherise.

And when Jessica stood up at the end, there was still a small crowd around the signing area.

"Thank you all for coming," she said to them. "This was a wonderful night, and I'm so happy that I got to meet you all. Enjoy the book!"

The crowd applauded her, and then we got out of there.

"Where are we going?" I asked.

"Fat Annie's," she said.

Burgers and beer.

A good choice.

I only wished, in that moment, that I could have the beer.

I'd just have to be satisfied with the burgers.

SEVENTEEN

Fat Annie's was this red, white, and blue monstrosity of a burger and beer joint. I think the color scheme was designed to keep you from staying too long. The burgers and the beer were astounding, but for some reason, we never had more than a second beer, even when I was drinking heavily. The place was just too bright.

They had dartboards and pool tables, but most people came for the food.

We ordered our burgers, mine a super-giant bacon burger with cheese, hers the slim and single burger with lots of veggies. To drink, she ordered a pint of a dark beer whose name I didn't catch. I ordered water.

"So," she said as we sat down at our table, "you're still sober."

"Yup," I said.

"I'm proud of you," she said. "What's it been, now? Five years?"

"Six."

"I'm more than proud," she said. "I'm impressed."

"Thanks. It's hard right now, though. I'm staring at that beer of yours and thinking how good it would taste."

She pulled it back from me instinctively, though just an inch.

"Should I have not ordered it?" She wore a real look of concern.

"Nah, you're fine. It's just been a difficult few months, and today, I had an argument with Mike."

"So that's what you wanted to talk about at the signing, but couldn't."

I took a sip of my water. It was cold and refreshing, but tasted nowhere near as good as that beer Jessica was guarding.

I couldn't have it, though, even if she would let me.

One drink, and I'd be done. I wouldn't be able to stop.

"Yeah," I said when I set my water back down.

"Tell me."

She took a sip of her beer, and I tried not to pay attention.

So I told her everything that happened at what was supposed to be a celebratory dinner. I was interrupted when the waitress came around with our food, but unlike Elise's pal Benny, she didn't hang around.

She either didn't know who we were, or she didn't care. Sometimes, I amuse myself with how disappointed I get at not being recognized, even though I would have preferred not to be recognized, most of the time.

Once I finished the story, we sat across from each other, taking bites of our burgers and eating in silence for a couple minutes.

"So the gist of this tale," Jessica said, "is that you just now figured out Mike is all about the money, and you're pissed off that you didn't figure it out sooner."

When she put it that way, I leaned my head back, looked at the ceiling, and laughed. Jessica always saw to the heart of the matter.

When I was done, I looked at her, took a bite of my burger, and nodded while I chewed. I waited until I swallowed before I responded with words.

"That pretty much sums it up."

"Any thoughts on what you're going to do?"

"Not a clue," I said. "I mean, I'm going to do the shows this weekend, of course, but I don't know what I'm going to do after that. I wasn't planning on staying."

Jessica bit into her burger, and a drop of juice dribbled down the side of her chin. She wiped it away, deftly, with a napkin.

"Do you even want to stay in music?" she asked.

"Of course," I said without thinking about it.

But the question bounced around inside my head even after I answered it. Did I want to remain a musician? It's what I had done my whole life, up until Johnny B.

"Really? You haven't done anything at all since Savage Anarchy. Not until Mike brought you this gig."

"I don't know what else I would do. Maybe I could get a job here."

"I can't see you in the uniform," she said.

I glanced over at one of the workers, a mildly overweight guy in blue pants, a white shirt, and a red tie. I tried to picture myself getting into that outfit. I couldn't.

"Alright. So not here. Maybe there's something else. I could write a book."

"I didn't ask because I thought you should quit and do something else," she said. "I asked because you don't seem to know what you're doing. You're adrift at the moment. You're going with whatever comes your way, and that's not any way to live your life. Especially not for the absolutely incredible guitar player you are."

"I don't get it," I said.

Jessica put her burger down, and then leaned forward.

"Okay, let me put it another way. Fuck Mike. You don't need him. He enabled your drinking."

"He helped get me out of it," I said.

"And then he stuck you in Savage Anarchy, which was about as dysfunctional a group of people as I've ever met. I'm surprised you lasted as long as you did with them. Hell, I'm surprised you didn't start drinking again."

I think most people who knew the story were surprised with that.

"Yes," Jessica continued. "He made you a lot of money, but look at where you're at now. You haven't chosen anything for yourself in years. Take control of your life. Don't let Mike run it for you."

Words. They were just words, but they rang through me like church bells.

"But what do I do about this situation? What if Rose hates me now?"

"Do what you want," she said. "If Rose hates you, that's not your fault. I think you did the right thing, telling her. She'd find out eventually, and the earlier she learns what you think, the sooner she can deal with it. But it's her problem, not yours."

Jessica's face grew a mischievous grin.

"And why would you care, anyway?" she asked. "You've only known her two days."

Why did I care? It's not like we had been friends for life. Rose was just...

Just what?

I didn't have an answer.

I shrugged my shoulders.

"I don't know why," I said. "I just know that what Mike is going to do to her, what he's trying to do to her and the band, isn't fair. They're good players. They just need to learn to write songs."

"And how do they do that?" Jessica asked.

"By writing songs," I said.

"Maybe you should tell that to Rose when you see her tomorrow."

"Yeah," I said. "Maybe I should."

But what did it matter? I didn't think she'd listen to me.

Jessica and I chatted for a while longer. She finished her beer, glanced at her watch, and then called it a night.

I don't remember most of the rest of the conversation. I could only think about what was to come the next day, and what I was going to do.

I barely even remember the drive home. I didn't even take my guitar out of the van, I was so lost in thought.

Jessica had raised some good questions and got me to think.

I didn't have any answers as I went to sleep.

EIGHTEEN

I arrived at the rehearsal studio just as everyone else did. The mood was certainly not as light as it had been before the disrupted dinner the previous night. Even Elise seemed to have lost quite a bit of her spunk.

Thankfully, Mike wasn't present.

I wasn't sure what I would have done had he showed his face.

I thought about it all night and realized that Jessica was right. I didn't actually owe Rose and the girls anything but as good a performance as I could produce. I hadn't done anything wrong in revealing Mike's opinion of the band's own songwriting skills. If Rose chose to be upset at me about it, then that's what she chose, and there was little I could do about it. At least she knew the truth.

Once we were in the room, the discussion centered completely around the mechanical necessity of moving their gear to the club. No one talked about what had happened last night. When I told Rose that I would just use my own gear at the show, she only said, "That's fine." She didn't even ask why.

So I helped Adelle pack up her drums, which obviously pleased her.

We carried everything out and packed it into a covered trailer that Rose owned. It, like the couch in the rehearsal room, was a bright pink color, clearly freshly washed. Stenciled on the side, the word 'October'. I finally knew the name of the band.

Eventually, we were standing around the trailer as Rose brought the last of the gear out and stuffed it inside.

Rose shut the door, and locked it.

"Adelle, will you drive it over?" she asked.

"Sure, why?"

"I need to talk to Trent," she said.

"Ooohhh," Adelle said.

"Adelle..."

"Yeah, I'll drive."

"Thanks," Rose said, then she came over to me. "I'm riding with you."

"Okay," I said.

Just like that, the group dispersed, and Rose followed me to my van.

Once we were inside, I went to start it up, but Rose put out her hand and said, "Hold on a minute."

I took my hand off the key, sat back in my chair, and turned to face Rose. This was where I was going to learn how Rose reacted to what I said. This was where I was going to have to make a decision, if the decision hadn't been made for me. I'd hoped not to have to worry about it until after the weekend was over.

"Did you really mean what you said about our songs?" she asked.

Straight to the point, which I liked. The hard question, I didn't like.

"I did," I said. It was too late to lie to her. Besides, the explanations for lying would be worse than knowing the reality.

"And Mike?" she asked with a quaver in her voice. For the first time, she almost sounded vulnerable.

"Yeah. He specifically wanted me to stay on and improve the quality of the songwriting."

"And you said..."

"I said I'd think about it, after I had told him no, and he pestered me to change my mind."

She pondered that for a moment. Out of the corner of my eye, I saw the trailer leave the parking lot.

"You've known Mike a long time."

"Yeah, though I think I didn't really know him until yesterday."

"What do you mean?"

"Somehow, I never connected the dots. I never saw him for what he was, until yesterday."

She took a deep breath.

"Are you still planning to leave after this weekend?"

In my head, I was still unsettled. I couldn't figure out what I wanted. Jessica had had some good points, the night before, about taking control of my life and not letting anyone run it for me. If I stayed, Rose would run a lot of it. It was her band, her rules, her identity.

If I left, well, then I'd have to find another band, or make one. And I wasn't sure I wanted to do that. It would be hard to put together a group of people that were as tight as this group.

"Yes," I said, knowing Rose needed an answer.

I don't know why I expected her to ask me to stay. Something in her mood, something I wanted?

"Okay," she said, and settled back in her seat. "Let's get to the club."

It wasn't at all what I expected.

The mood in the air between us shifted just like that, from intimate, to business.

It was like she had decided to give up and just do what's in front of her.

I could respect that.

But I didn't know what to make of it.

I started the van, put it in gear, and set us on our way to the night's event.

NINETEEN

At the club, the afternoon was all business.
Setup.

Sound check.

A quick rehearsal that went well and seemed to lift the malaise that had hung over us since the night before.

Another sound check.

And then it was time for dinner.

The club made some delicious pizzas, which was the one thing I remembered being good about the place, before they started hiring real acts. And the pizzas were still good.

We sat around a table in the corner, eating pizza and chatting about inane things, avoiding the harder topics like Mike and whether I was staying or going. It was a group of friends chatting about shit. A way to pass the time.

Carol pestered Elise about Benny, the waiter, asking Elise if she was ever going to let the guy go out with her. Adelle sat close to me and wanted stories of the Narc Souls days, which I gave her—though I steered away from the meat, only giving her the dessert stories. Rose chimed in on both conversations, but pretty much stayed away from getting deeply involved.

She still had things on her mind.

Including, I suspected, wondering where Mike was.

I was also a bit surprised Mike hadn't made an appearance. I thought he would have wanted to see the support his new pet project had received due to his promotional efforts, but none of us had heard even a word from him since the night before.

If I knew him, he had his reasons, like not wanting to upset the talent before a show, or some such nonsense.

He couldn't make me any more upset than I already was, and I would have put money on it that Rose felt the same.

Either way, whether he was there or not, he was a source of tension, at least for Rose and myself.

As we ate, Ross Egan, the manager of the Showcase, came to our table. He was a heavy-set guy of average height. He'd shaved his head since the last time I saw him, and he had far more lines around his eyes, but he had the same smiling visage that I remembered. He'd be your best friend as long as you were bringing money into his club. If no one showed for your gigs, though, out you went.

"Trent," he said. "Haven't seen you around here in a long time. I was surprised to hear you were playing with the girls, but I'm glad you are. Two sold out shows! I couldn't have asked for a better gift."

Same old Ross. Always, and obviously, about the money.

I glanced at Rose, expecting to see a glare, and Ross would have deserved it, but Rose was keeping her expression neutral, which was probably for the best.

I stood up and shook Ross's hand. I expected the same flabby handshake that I remembered, considering Ross's excess girth hadn't changed, but his handshake was strong and firm.

"It's been a long time, hasn't it." And then I remembered something that Mike had said when he got me to sign on for the gig. "I thought this place had new owners."

Ross's grin grew even bigger.

"I'm the new owner, baby! I bought this place out with some money I had set aside and started running it the way I wanted to run it."

"Congratulations," I said. "You seem to be doing well."

"Eh, we have good days and bad. It's looking like this weekend is going to be good, though! Who would have thought, when I booked this gig, that I'd have Trent Richards on the bill?"

Not me, certainly. Not the girls, either.

I glanced down at Rose.

Her neutral mask had broken, and her fuming interior was showing through.

I had to end the conversation quickly. Ross's excitement for the weekend was all about me, and not about the band. It was, probably, exactly what Mike had hoped for.

And as much as we didn't like it, Rose and I were stuck with it.

"Well, as much as I'd like it to be about me," I said, "it's really about the band. I'm just here to fill in for the weekend."

"Sure you are, but you chose to do it at my place, and you're playing all the old Narcoleptic Souls songs. These girls are really good, but I long for the old Narc Souls. Any chance of you getting them back together?"

Out of the corner of my eye, I saw that the others all wore sour faces, now. This was getting out of hand, and I had to end it.

"I don't think that's ever going to happen," I said. "Look Ross, it's good to see you, and maybe we can talk a little later, but I've got to get back into the dressing room and prepare for the show."

"Sure, sure," he said. "Always good to see you. Whenever you decide on your next gig, make sure you bring it here."

We shook hands again, and then he walked off. He wasn't five feet away before he started shouting across the room at one of his employees.

I turned to Rose, who had somehow managed to hide the turmoil inside, again. If I didn't have an idea of how I'd feel in her place, I would not have been able to guess.

"Look, I'm sorry," I said. "I didn't..."

"It's not your fault he's an asshole," she said, "or that you are who you are."

"Still..."

"It's no big deal. Let's go get ready for the show."

"You sure?"

"I'm sure."

And, as if to prove it, she stood up and started off across the empty dance floor toward the dressing room.

The others stood as she left.

"She's right," Elise said, patting me on the shoulder as she walked by. "This isn't your fault."

But I couldn't help feeling that I held some responsibility. I wasn't sure what I could have done differently, but there had to be something.

I followed the girls into the dressing room, and then stopped with my hand holding the door open.

Rose was in the center of the room, her shirt already off. She stood with her back to me. Her back was well muscled, but not overly so, something I had not been able to see with the clothes she had worn the last couple days. Where the black bra strap crossed wrapped around her sides, it did not bite into her skin.

She turned around, and while I couldn't see her nipples under her bra, I couldn't help but imagine them. I couldn't help but imagine her breasts unleashed from that bra.

I turned away, though not all the way around.

"In or out, Trent," she said, "but don't hold the door open."

Elise and the others turned to look at me, and Elise started laughing. The others did, too.

"Look," Adelle said. "He's blushing."

Fuck.

No. What the hell?

But she was right. I could feel the heat in my face.

I've seen plenty of naked women, and I can't remember the last time I blushed. And Rose wasn't even naked. It was all in my head.

Except that she was standing in the room with her hands wrapped around the shirt she had just taken off, waiting for me to decide whether to stay in, or go outside.

I shut the door, and stayed inside.

If she and the others were okay with me being in the room, then I would be okay, too.

I turned back to face the girls, who were all smiling. Even Rose had a bit of a smile.

"I guess we never considered this issue," Rose said.

I know I hadn't considered it. I'd only been thinking about the show and how Mike was taking advantage of everyone.

I looked around the room.

It wasn't exactly large—no bigger than the size of a smallish master bedroom.

On the wall to my right hung a large mirror above a counter top with three short stools below it. An old, beat up recliner sat in another corner of the room, and there were a half dozen open closets on the wall opposite the mirror.

If I stayed, the quarters would be tight.

"What do you think, Elise?" Rose asked.

"If he wants to stay, I don't mind," she said. "It'll be funny to watch him squirm if he's going to blush like that all the time."

"I think you should stay, Trent," Adelle said. "After all, you've got to change, too, and I'd really like to see what's underneath."

They all laughed.

If I couldn't keep my face under control, then what about other parts of me? Even the thought of staying was stirring feelings which could put me in a terribly embarrassing situation.

"Carol?" Rose asked.

"I'm okay with it. If he's going to be in the band, he ought to be part of the band."

And that was an issue that hit home.

Was I going to be in the band?

I kept saying no.

Was it right for me to act like I was in the band when I wasn't?

"You know," I said. "I think it's probably better if I wait outside until you're all dressed."

I put my hand on the doorknob.

"No," Rose said. "You stay."

Stay.

They all wanted me to stay.

Even after what Mike said at dinner, even after what I told Rose about the songwriting, she wanted me to stay.

I didn't think I could do it.

"I don't think it's a good idea," I said.

"Why not?" Rose asked.

"Look, I like you and all, and the rehearsals were good, but I got out of Savage Anarchy because I couldn't handle dealing with all the bullshit. I'm pretty sure my drinking while in Narc Souls stemmed from the same issues.

"I'm just not good in a group."

And it felt true, as I said it. I'd never admitted it aloud before, and I'd never made the connection between the drinking and the bullshit of being in a band before.

And I'd certainly never connected any of it with Mike before the unfortunate situation at Georgio's.

It also felt distinctively odd having four girls who I respected for their musical talent ask me to stay in the room while they changed clothes.

"You don't even know," Elise said. "Rose told us all about Mike and how he manipulated the bands you were in. She told us about why he wanted you to join us. We're all cool with it."

I took my hand off the doorknob, and turned to fully face them.

"You didn't go home," I said, looking straight at Rose. "You went back to Georgio's and told them what I said."

"I did," she said. "They needed to know, and I needed to talk about it."

"And you still want me to stay. You all want me to stay. Even after the way Ross behaved out there? You would think you didn't even exist, the way he ignored you all."

The four of them seemed to pass messages between their brains through their eyes. They talked without talking, had a long discussion with me in the room, unable to hear.

And then they looked at me again.

"Yes," Rose said. "Ross's behavior isn't your fault. It does hurt, but we understand it. It's just the same shit that Mike is doing to us. For them, it's all about money."

"Bunch of assholes," Adelle said under her breath.

"The truth," Carol said.

"I realized last night," Rose continued, "when you were telling me what Mike wanted, that money wasn't what you were about."

"You don't know that," I said. "I only took the gig because Mike was going to get me three grand."

"But if it was just about money," Rose said, "you wouldn't have argued with Mike, you wouldn't have told me his plans, and you wouldn't be conflicted about staying."

Then, unexpectedly, she dropped her shirt off to the side, and stepped close enough to me that all I could see was her face. We stood only inches apart.

Her eyes locked on mine, and I couldn't help but look deep into them, even as I felt she was seeing my soul through mine.

"I've been watching you. When you play, you get lost in the music. You close your eyes and just play. For you, it's all about the music."

I could feel the heat of her breath on my neck as she spoke.

I suddenly had a desire to wrap my arms around her, pull her close, hug her tight.

"How can you be sure?" I asked, firmly keeping my desires in check.

"Why do you protest?"

"You didn't want me in the band," I said.

"I didn't want a drunk in the band. I didn't want someone who couldn't control himself in the band. I didn't want someone who would pick fights in the band."

"And you thought I was all of those," I said.

"I did. What did I have to go on but the publicity generated by the things that you did, or had done to you?"

"I don't know."

"I loved your music, but the public image you projected was that of an asshole." Her voice was warm, soft. It wasn't the angry Rose that I had met the first day.

"You know," I said, wanting to put distance between us, "you've only known me for three days. You don't really know me. I may not be drinking, but I'm still that alcoholic. I survived not drinking with Savage Anarchy on pure guts and stubbornness, and even then, I didn't survive. I walked out because I couldn't handle it anymore. I don't know if I could handle it now, and I don't want to fuck up your band. I don't want to be that person anymore, yet I'm already doing it again. My last girlfriend left me because I just can't seem to pull my head out of my ass."

"Shut up," Rose said in the harshest tone she possessed. Her face tightened up in anger, but it still, somehow, showed some compassion that I hadn't imagined existed in her.

"I..."

"Shut up, I said. You are not a fuck-up. People who play like you aren't fuck-ups. People who write music that moves people the way you do aren't fuck-ups. We wouldn't want you to stay if you were a fuck-up.

"The fact that you argued for us and our vision proved to me that you are, in fact, a good person who's had some shit luck. That you told me what Mike's plans were proves you have some integrity that most guys in this business that I've met don't have.

"We all want you in the band. We want you to stay. Teach us what you know about writing songs. Help us get out of this tribute band gig."

I tore my eyes away from Rose and searched the faces of the others. I found the same thing in each of them—an anticipation of my answer, a desire for me to say yes.

But something held me back. I couldn't say yes. Not then. Memories of Mike beseeching Johnny B. to take me into Savage Anarchy surfaced, and it felt the same way. Back then, I was looking for a way to prove myself, again. I wanted to prove that I wasn't a drunk.

And the idea of stepping back into that was too big, and they were all waiting for me to say yes.

Even with Rose standing there, nearly topless, and my desire for her peaking, the desire to run away was right there. I couldn't do it again. I couldn't fail again.

But I couldn't say no to her, either.

"Let's just play the shows this weekend. I want to see how they go. I'll help you learn to write better songs, if you want, but I don't know if I can handle staying in the band."

The girls stayed silent, but I could almost hear their sighs of disappointment.

"I mean, I appreciate the offer to stay. I do. I know it's not coming from Mike, and that means a lot. It's just that I'm a mess right now, and I don't want to be a burden in the future."

"You wouldn't be a burden," Adelle said.

Rose stepped back a little, helping me to relax.

"I don't know that," I said. "Let's just see how the weekend goes."

"Okay," Rose said. "I understand."

"Thank you," I said. I put my hand on the doorknob again. "I'll be right outside. Let me know when you're done changing."

And then I opened the door, stepped out into the hallway, and let the door shut behind me.

I leaned up against the wall, took a deep breath, and shut my eyes while I waited.

I needed to sort out what the hell was going on inside me, but I didn't feel like I had any time.

TWENTY

Two hours later, I stood at the end of the hallway, behind a curtain that separated me from the crowd outside. The opening act, a new band that I thought had promise, had just finished and were pulling their gear off the stage.

Everyone talks about butterflies in their stomach when they're nervous, but I didn't have butterflies. I had bumblebees in mine, bouncing around at insane speeds. It was making me sick, and I felt like I wanted to throw up.

But I wasn't going to do that.

Part of me realized that I was going to do something I hadn't done in over a year, and part of me realized that the last time I had been staring out at a crowd like this was when Johnny B. had punched me.

There wasn't any chance the girls were going to go all MMA on me, but I couldn't keep the flashback from running through my head, again and again.

"You all right?" Carol asked from behind me. She nearly shouted the question. The crowd was already working itself up.

"Yeah, I'm good," I said.

"You look nervous."

"You're supposed to ignore that."

Carol smiled.

"Rose sent you to check up on me."

"Yes," she said.

"Tell her I'm fine. I'll be good as soon as we go on stage. I always get nervous before a show."

"Okay, I'll tell her," Carol said, but she made no move to leave.

A couple minutes passed while we stood there watching the other band clear their gear. On one hand, I wished she would leave, but on the other, it was nice to be standing there with someone, too. In less than fifteen minutes, I'd be playing my first show in forever, and having her there beside me meant I wasn't doing it alone.

"The crowd's pretty big," Carol said, breaking into the din.

It was big for the Showcase. The place was packed.

"Is this the largest crowd you've played for?" I asked.

"No. We played a festival last year, one of a dozen bands, and there were more people there. They weren't there to hear us, though."

Just like now, I thought. The crowd wasn't there to listen to them, they were there for me.

And it wasn't fair.

"Fuck Mike," I said.

"What?" Carol asked.

"Fuck Mike. Why the hell did he do this to me?"

"Do what?"

"Why did he put me in this position? Why did he have to tell everyone that I was playing guitar for you? Why couldn't he just let me play and be invisible? Why the fuck did he have to make such a big deal out of it?"

Carol did the safe thing and stayed quiet. None of us had any answers, and Mike wasn't there.

"He should fucking be here," I said. "He should have been here an hour ago."

"Maybe he's afraid to show up?"

I shook my head.

"No, that's not it. He probably doesn't want to give me any opportunity to tell him to go fuck himself."

"I'd like to see that," she said.

The band finished clearing the stage, and the house sound engineer and his assistant were busy checking our mics.

Only a few minutes left.

I really wanted to see Mike before the show. I wanted to tell him how pissed off I was.

But that wasn't going to happen.

There wasn't any time.

I felt the others come up behind Carol and I.

I turned around to see them.

They all wore the dark makeup around the eyes that had been the hallmark of Narcoleptic Souls. On Rose and Adelle, their deep dark eyes nearly disappeared and gave them a bit of a demonic look. I'd noticed it somewhat in the dressing room, but out here in the hallway, where the light was a little dimmer, their makeup gave them a far more forbidding look than I had expected.

"Trent," Rose said. "We usually stand in a circle, put our hands in the center, and someone says a few words before we go on."

I nodded, and I understood. They were a team, like a band should be.

She put her hand out.

The others waited, though.

They all stared at me.

"You're next," Elise said.

I hesitated, and Carol nodded.

I put my hand in, on top of Rose's. Her hand was warm to the touch. I instantly wanted to wrap my hand around hers, but I resisted the urge.

Adelle put hers in next, on top of mine, then Elise, then Carol.

"This show is for us," Rose said. Then she looked directly at me. "It's also for you, Trent. Even if you don't stay on after this weekend, for now, you're one of us."

I nodded, understanding. This was the way a band should be.

"Play like you mean it, girls."

Then she laughed.

"I guess that doesn't really work this weekend, does it?"

It broke some of the nervousness inside me. This woman who was so focused on her band, the moment before a show that could turn out to be a disaster for them, could laugh, too. She wasn't all about the pressure to be good.

"Why not?" I asked. "Tonight, I'm one of you, right?"

"Damn straight!" Elise said.

And then they all pushed in for a group hug. They pulled me in, too.

TWENTY-ONE

The crowd yelled and shouted when the girls took the stage, but it went to another level when I climbed up the steps. This wasn't the girls' crowd. This was my crowd.

I hated Mike for it, and I felt bad for the girls, but they were ignoring what it meant as best they could.

I picked up my guitar, strapped it on, felt the familiar bite of the strings under my fingertips.

Adelle cracked her sticks together four times.

We hit the first note hard and loud, and the lights came up. I shut my eyes, and I played.

It was as good as I remembered, only better, because I didn't really remember that many of the shows from my Narc Souls days.

Right there, on that stage, I felt what it was like to really be in a band again, and it was easy to fit right in, especially since the first few songs were all songs I had written.

When the first song finished, the crowd roared, but we didn't wait to listen to it. We launched right into the next song.

And after that, for the next half hour, I did nothing but play and bask in the glory of the music.

And then we played the first of their original songs.

The crowd quieted, the energy dropped.

They didn't know what they were listening to.

The girls could feel it, too.

Rose, in particular, looked at me. I couldn't tell what she was thinking, the way the eye shadow hid her eyes, but I felt pretty sure she wasn't happy.

And then we segued into another Narc Souls song, and the energy of the crowd picked up again.

It happened that way every time we played one of their own songs, and then followed it with a Narc Souls song.

And every time, Rose looked at me as if she wanted me to tell her something, or pass judgment, or, I don't know. Tell her it was okay.

We ended the show with three Narc Souls songs in a row, the last of them, *Rise Above Anger*. And we played it like we had in the first rehearsal. Magic flowed from our arms, fingertips, and vocal chords. The crowd felt it. I felt it.

Whatever else may have transpired before then, whatever else would transpire after, that performance of that song would live on in all of the minds of those who were there.

When we played the last note and the last cymbal crash died away, we stood in front of the crowd together, in a line, arms around each other. I couldn't breathe. The crowd writhed and cheered. They started chanting.

We bowed.

Then we left the stage and returned to the dressing room.

For the moment, I was one of them. I belonged in the band, and nowhere else.

And it all came crashing down when I walked through the dressing room door and saw Mike standing next to another man, right inside the doorway.

I knew the man. His follicle-challenged head and wire-rimmed glasses and hollow-cheeked face were instantly recognizable to anyone who followed the music industry.

Roman Harper. The founder of Harper Pacific Recording Company—the largest record company in the industry.

I probably could have seen it coming, should have seen it coming. Mike had a plan, all along.

He hadn't made himself visible prior to the show because he didn't want to stir the pot. He wanted to spring Mr. Harper on us, overwhelm the girls and myself.

It was working on the girls. Harper was all over the music industry news. He didn't hide in his office, and it was well known that he scouted talent for himself.

Rose, Adelle, Carol, and Elise were all excited, shaking his hand, hopping up and down in disbelief. Having Roman Harper at the show was more than they could have asked for, and here he was, telling them all how wonderful the show was, how stunning they were.

I didn't want to enter the room, but I did, anyway. A surprising desire to protect the girls, and Rose, overcame my desire to ditch the whole thing and go home.

I went right to Roman and shook his hand.

"Roman," I said.

"Trent. How're you doing? Great show."

"Did Mike drag you out here to see us?" I asked.

"I don't know if the term, 'dragged', is accurate. I've always liked to watch you play. When Mike mentioned you had joined a new group, I had to come see. I couldn't let anyone else have a chance at you first, now could I?"

"I suppose not," I said. "Though, I think you might have misunderstood the situation. I'm only filling in for their regular guitar player."

He kept his eyes on me, instead of glancing away at Mike like I thought he might.

"Oh? That would be a shame. You all played so well together, it was like you'd been working together for years."

And it was like that, at least on the Narc Souls songs.

"Just a couple of days," I said.

"Impressive. Well, don't let me keep you from getting cleaned up. I just wanted to let you know what I thought."

"Thanks," I said, then stepped away to go to my closet.

I pulled out a towel that I kept in my bag, and started wiping the sweat off my face with it. Even if the Showcase had provided towels, I wouldn't have trusted how clean they would be.

On the counter sat a large cooler filled with bottles of water and other drinks, half of which were alcoholic. I wound my way over to it, and as tempting as it was to choose the alcohol, I pulled a bottle of water from the chest. I opened it and took a long drink, enjoying the chill of it as it worked its way down my throat.

Someone knocked at the door. When Elise opened it to find Benny, the waiter, standing there, Elise jumped into his arms. It seemed there really was something between them.

I spent a moment taking in the action around the room.

Carol was lounging in the recliner, Adelle against the wall next to her. Elise pulled Benny into the room and shut the door. Mike and Roman stood talking to each other, drinks in their hands.

And Rose.

Rose stood on the other side of the room from me, watching like I was.

She had wiped the makeup from her eyes, though there were streaks where she had missed some of it. Whatever excitement she'd had upon initially meeting Roman, it had drained away.

I grabbed another bottle of water, and made my way to Rose. Her eyes followed me.

"Here," I said and handed her the bottle.

She took it.

"Thanks," she said as she twisted off the top.

She put the bottle to her lips and took a long pull off of it.

"Good show," I said. "It's been a long time for me."

"Change your mind?" she asked.

"Can we maybe not talk about that?" I asked. I didn't even want to think about where it all was going right then. Mike and Roman were too close for me to want to talk about it freely. I could almost feel them staring at me.

"Sure," she said, "though it's totally amazing that Roman Harper showed up." Her voice did not convey the same excitement as her words.

But it was clear that she couldn't not talk about it. In the heat of the moment, the glow of a good show, it was hard not to think of the possibilities, especially when the man himself showed up to watch.

I didn't think we could have any sort of real conversation with Mike and Roman in the room. As much as she was angry about Mike, he'd found the right way to keep her in the fold.

And, years ago, it would have kept me in the fold, too.
But not this time. Not any more.
"How about we go somewhere quiet," I said.
"Where?"
"I don't know, but I want to get out of here."
She tilted her head, slightly.
"I know a place," she said
"Where?"
"You drive, I'll tell you how to get there."

TWENTY-TWO

We took my van after we gathered our guitars and our clothes. The amps would stay, but she felt like I did. It was the guitars themselves that were worth the money. They were what you protected.

Once we were away from the club, she directed me onto the freeway. Even at eleven at night, there was quite a bit of traffic until we got out of the city.

We drove north, then exited to a smaller highway that I knew led down to Mukilteo and the waters of Puget Sound.

"The ferry?" I asked.

"No," she said. "Turn left, up ahead."

I did as she said, and we found ourselves on a winding little road that switched back and forth as it descended down a steep hill.

The road ended at the bottom in a cul-de-sac. There were obvious plots for houses, but they had never been built upon.

"Park it," she said.

I did, and we got out. It was cold. Surrounded by trees as we were, we couldn't see the water, but we could hear it, and the wind blew off the water and through the trees.

"Do you have a blanket in this thing?" she asked.

I did. I had moving blankets to keep my equipment from being dinged, but they would work to keep us warm. I pulled a couple out of the back and locked up the van.

"Charming," she said. "Follow me."

Then she led me off into the woods.

We walked maybe a quarter mile before we emerged from the trees atop a rise above the water. There wasn't any beach, as the tide was in.

Off to our right was a fallen tree that looked like it had lain there for years.

"Over there," she said.

"By the tree?"

"Yeah, I like to sit there and watch the lights from the island twinkle off the water."

The water was black. The lights on the other side of the water came from Whidbey Island. I didn't see any twinkle, though.

She led me over to the tree, and sat down with her back against it.

I handed her one of the blankets, and she covered herself with it.

I sat down next to her, and covered myself with the other blanket.

"You know," she said, "out here, it's easier to think. There aren't any demands. No pressure. Just me, the water, and the trees."

"The island?"

"It's over there," she said, pushing out with her arm. "It can't hurt us, and it doesn't talk. It just does its thing, uncaring of what I might be thinking."

"So why are we out here?" I asked.

"You wanted to go somewhere quiet, and this is the quietest place I know. Besides, you looked like you could use some serenity. You can't get that in the city."

"No," I said. "You can't."

For awhile, we listened to the sound of the waves.

Eventually, she broke the silence.

"So why did you want to go somewhere quiet?"

"I couldn't stay, not with Mike and Roman in the room."

"Mike's still got you pissed off, doesn't he?"

"It's more than that. I can see what he's doing, and I don't like it."

"I see what he's doing, too, you know."

I turned my head toward her just enough so that I could see her out of the corner of my eye. She still faced the water, staring out into the dark.

"Tell me," I said.

"He wants you in this band. He wants your name on it so that he'll make money. You're almost a guaranteed draw. He brought Roman in to try to get you to change your mind about leaving after tomorrow. Am I right?"

"Pretty much," I said.

"And I think I understand where you're coming from, too."

"You do? We hardly know each other."

She turned and looked at me, then. It was too dark to see her face clearly, but I thought I saw compassion in her eyes.

"My dad was a writer. He did it practically in his sleep. He couldn't stop. But he always railed about how little they paid him. He wrote these cheap, dime a dozen, action books for men. He never had a breakout book, but they always made a crapload of money for the publisher. Every time he wanted to quit writing them and work on what he thought he should be writing, they sweetened the pot just enough to keep him working on those shitty action books."

"What happened?"

Rose didn't even hesitate.

"Eventually, he drank himself to death without ever writing the books he wanted to write."

"Oh, I'm sorry. I..."

"You don't have to be sorry. He died years ago, and we weren't talking about him. We were talking about you."

"Me?"

"You're just like him, though you've had more success."

"I'm not drinking, though."

"No, you're not. Not right now. But have you been doing what you're supposed to be doing? Have you been writing songs, playing music? Have you been in control of your work?"

I couldn't say yes. I couldn't say anything.

"You've let Mike run your career. You've let him bribe you into doing things you don't want to. You can't let him do that."

Out on the Sound, the lights of a ferry reflected off the water. I watched its slow traversal of the Sound as it crossed to Whidbey Island while I tried to accept what she was saying.

I knew it was the truth. I'd figured it out sometime between the fight with Mike and planting my ass on the beach next to Rose, but admitting it was difficult.

"What are you thinking?" Rose asked.

"I know you're telling me the truth," I said. "I haven't got a clue what to do about it, though. You all seem to want me to stay, but by staying, I'd be giving in to him, wouldn't I?"

"Only if you stayed because he wanted you to. What do *you* want to do?"

"I don't know. I just know I don't want to deal with Mike and his bullshit."

"You wouldn't have to," she said. "We could find another manager."

She was offering to drop Mike. I couldn't believe it.

"You would do that? Mike's the best. He brought Roman Harper to your show. You've got a chance..."

"We don't have a chance without you," she said, sounding resigned.

"Sure you do. You're all amazing players."

"I saw the reactions of the crowd tonight when we played our songs. I've seen them before, but I always put them down to the crowd not knowing the songs.

"But I really paid attention tonight. You and Mike are right. There's something missing, and we don't know what it is."

The wind picked up and made things chillier than they were, even under the blankets.

"I don't have to be with the band to help you learn how to write better songs. It really just comes down to writing more of them. As many as you can."

"If only it were so easy," she said.

The pressure I was feeling inside me started to ease as the topic of the conversation changed, and became about her. This was something I could talk about without having to think about the turmoil I wanted to avoid.

"I wrote hundreds of songs before I joined Narc Souls," I said. "Most of them weren't any good."

"We don't have the time to write that many songs," she said.

"Sure you do," I said. "You've just got to make the time."

"Tell me, genius, if you were us, how would you make the time?"

"Stop playing Narc Souls songs. Stop playing the tribute gigs. Use the time to write songs. Build yourself up. Stop pretending to be someone else."

She sat up straight, then leaned in so that our faces were no more than six inches apart.

"You know..."

"I know. My advice applies to my situation, too."

"It does."

She leaned a little closer. Even in the wind, I felt her breath on my lips.

"We weren't kidding, earlier," she said. "We want you in the band. We talked about it after you told me what Mike wanted from you, and we agreed that it was best if we could convince you to stay."

"But..."

She put her finger to my lips. It had a few grains of sand on it, but I ignored them.

"I know what you're going to say. I know you don't know what you want. I know you're afraid that we're being manipulated by Mike and his promises. And you're probably afraid that you'll screw up this band, too."

I nodded, but her finger was still on my lips, and I didn't want it to move, so I didn't say anything.

"You won't screw it up. We made this decision, and Mike wasn't involved. We even talked about giving Mike the kick in the ass he deserves, and we agreed that if we had to do it, we would.

"But we all want this, more than anything. We want you in the band, and it's not because of your fame. Something magical happens when we play the Narc Souls songs with you, and we want that magic for our own songs. You fit with us, and there's no one we'd rather have."

It was quite a change from the first day.

"What about you?"

"Me?"

"You hated me that first day," I said. "You didn't want me anywhere near the band. Now..."

"I was just surprised. I only knew you by your reputation. Now, I want you in the band. I want you to teach us how to write music. I want to write songs with you. I'm not the fangirl that Adelle is, but..."

It was my turn to put my finger to her lips. I couldn't have this turn into Candi.

"I don't need to hear what a fan of mine you are. It only gets in the way. I'm staying away from fans, these days. It never works out."

She sat back.

"What? You think I..." She was trying to sound indignant, but there was a note in her voice that said she was only a half second away from laughing.

"I would never," I said, also faux indignantly.

But I realized that I was hoping she would, even though it would only make things that much more difficult if anything went wrong.

"You had better be lying," she said.

"Oh? And if I wasn't? Is my body the only reason you want me in the band?"

"You know it. All I've ever wanted was to sleep with you right here on this beach."

"Wait a minute." I attempted to look shocked. "Why are you here, Adelle? I thought I brought Rose."

Rose tilted her head and shaped her lips into the same sort of smile that Adelle always wore around me. Then she leaned in, just like Adelle would do. This time, though, she wasn't six inches from me, she was two.

"You can't tell us apart?"

Hot breath escaped her lips with the words.

"It's so hard," I said.

"It had better be," Rose said.

Her lips touched mine, soft and full, tentative at first, then with more pressure. She tasted like cherries.

When our tongues finally met, I forgot about the beach, the band, Candi, Mike, everything.

There was only Rose, and the beat of my heart, and her breath on my face, and the warmth of her body.

TWENTY-THREE

I awoke in my apartment to the sound of my phone ringing. Rose slept next to me, oblivious to the sound of the phone, which was probably just as well. We didn't get back to my apartment until nearly daybreak, and even then, we didn't fall right asleep.

The ring of the phone was insistent, so I sat up, swung my legs out of bed, bent down and searched the pockets of my jeans for my phone.

When I found it, I took it out of the room before I answered it. I didn't want to wake Rose.

"Hello?" I asked without even looking to see who it was.

"Trent," Mike's voice said on the other end. "What are you up to? This is the third time I've tried calling."

"I was sleeping," I said. "What do you want?"

"Do you know where Rose is? The girls are calling me to see if I know. It's after one, and they haven't heard from her."

Apparently, no one saw us slip out. I hadn't realized we were so stealthy.

"She's with me," I said. "We went for a drive last night and had a long talk about the band."

"Ah, good man. So you're staying?"

"No."

"No? I thought that her staying with you meant..."

I rolled my eyes, even though Mike couldn't see me do it. I wanted to slap him.

"Just because she's here, sleeping, doesn't mean anything happened. We went on a long drive, talked for a long time, and then had to crash someplace, and with her place all the way across town and the sun coming up, we decided just to crash at mine."

I hoped he believed the bullshit. We didn't do a lot of talking after that first kiss.

"So what, precisely, did you discuss about the band?"

"We talked about where she wanted to take the band, and we talked about how they could improve their song-writing. I don't have to be a part of the band in order to help them with that."

"But it's your chance to be part of something big, again," Mike said. "When I talked with Roman last night and told him that you would be doing the song writing, he was ready to sign you right there to a multi-album deal."

"What the hell, Mike? I haven't even agreed to stay in the band and you're already making deals?"

"Isn't that what you want? A chance to be huge, again? The five of you *would* be huge. All the ingredients are there."

"I don't want to be fucking huge," I said. "I want a life. One that's free from the bullshit that I had to deal with in Souls and Anarchy. What did it get me? The first time, it turned me into an alcoholic, the second time got me sucker-punched and turned into a pariah among the fans. Why would I want that again?"

"Because it's what you do," Mike said.

"It is *not* what I do."

I hung up.

I sat down on the couch.

I looked at my blank wall where the gold and platinum records had hung.

He couldn't be right.

Could he?

"Who was that?" Rose asked.

She stood in the doorway, her hair mussed, a blanket wrapped around her with her bare legs poking out from underneath it.

"Mike," I said.

"Oh."

She came over and sat down next to me.

"You're naked," she said.

I looked down. She was right. I hadn't even noticed.

I didn't move to cover up, though. I couldn't get the thought out of my head that Mike might be right. Could it be possible that what I was good at was turning a garage band into superstars, and then destroying it all in a meltdown?

I pointed at the wall.

"I used to have all my gold and platinum records hanging up there on the wall."

"Where'd you put them?"

"They're in storage," I said. "I couldn't stand to look at them anymore. They were always taunting me."

"Taunting you. How?"

"They were proof that whatever I did, I'd screw it up."

"That doesn't make a lot of sense," she said.

"I know, but sometimes, I don't make a lot of sense. I mean, who else can join a garage band, help it become hugely popular, and then fuck it all up?"

She leaned against me, and her hair tickled my shoulder.

"Maybe you're looking at it the wrong way."

"How do you mean?"

"Maybe those bands got what they wanted. They wanted to get big, and you gave it to them. Without you, maybe they would have been nothing. What happened at the end happens to most bands, so maybe it wasn't your fault at all."

"Even you blamed me for the end of Narc Souls," I said.

Her hand slipped out from under her blanket and came to rest on my leg. It wasn't sexual at all. It was comforting.

"I did," she said. "I still do. You *were* that band. You wrote all the music, wrote most of the lyrics. Without you, the rest of them were nothing."

"You're not doing a very good job explaining why it wasn't my fault."

"They would have *always* been nothing without you. They would have just been another garage band, maybe played the local club circuit, and then died after a couple years of not making it anywhere. My point is that they would have died, anyway."

"You don't know that," I said.

"Of course I do. If they could have lived without you, they would have been able to do it after you left. I blame you for ending that band, but everything they were was because of you.

"And what I missed most about the end of Narc Souls is

that I never got to hear more of your music."

"So you *are* a fangirl," I said, trying to lighten the mood. I didn't really want to continue talking about it. The whole subject gave me a deep desire to just shut down. I wanted to hide.

But Rose didn't take the hint.

"I got so excited when you joined Savage Anarchy. I thought I'd get to hear more of your music, but they wrote most of it. I could hear your influence, but it wasn't the same."

"Johnny would never have played any of my music," I said.

"If you want proof you didn't fuck it up, all you have to do is look at the fact that they released an album last month. They're still going strong."

"They're not doing as well, though. It barely registered on the charts."

"That's because you weren't there, but can you really blame yourself for that? You said Johnny never liked you. He was looking for his opportunity. You gave it to him. If your departure from Savage Anarchy was anyone's fault, it was his."

It was hard not to hear the logic in what she was saying, but it was also difficult not to reject it. I firmly believed that I was responsible for my actions, no matter what they were, and that one had to take responsibility for the actions and the consequences.

I was the one who turned to drinking, and I was the one who provoked Johnny B. If I hadn't done those things, maybe Narc Souls would still be a band, or maybe I wouldn't have had to sell the rights to my songs to cover my debts. Maybe I wouldn't be broke right now.

And maybe Rose wouldn't be sitting here next to me wanting me to take October to the same place I took the others.

The thought occurred to me that perhaps the only reason she had slept with me was to keep me in the band, to get me to stay. I instantly hated that I'd even had the thought, but it was there.

"What are you thinking?" she asked.

"I'm trying not to think," I said.

"Why?"

Her hand hadn't moved from my thigh, and we were both still staring straight ahead at the wall.

"Because I don't want to tell you. It's stupid, and it's probably wrong, and I'm certain it'll piss you off."

"Tell me." Her voice was still soft as butter—not the hard knife that she had used on me that first day.

"Promise me you won't get upset?"

"How can I promise that? I don't know what you're going to tell me."

She had a point.

I closed my eyes, preparing to tell her. I wasn't going to lie to her, but it was a stupid thought. Except that maybe it wasn't.

She pulled her hand away, and then quickly spun in her seat. I opened my eyes to find her looking straight at me. She didn't bother to keep the blanket shut, and I could see the inner curves of her breasts through the gap. I remembered holding them in my hands, caressing them, and in that moment, I could see how if I told her what I was thinking, I might never get that opportunity again. I could see how we might never speak again.

And I didn't want that to happen.

"Please don't tell me that you think I slept with you last night just to keep you in the band."

"I don't think that," I said.

"But the thought crossed your mind."

I forced myself to look up into her eyes.

"It did," I said.

"And would it matter if I actually did sleep with you just to get you to stay? Would it have changed anything?"

I had to think about it. Would I do anything differently if that was why she slept with me? I know I would have said 'no' earlier in my life. I would have just gone with it.

But after Candi, after the two bands, after what I'd come to realize about Mike and how he used me, I had trouble with the idea of saying no.

"Yes," I said. "If I knew that was why, it would matter."

"Would it make you stay?"

"No."

She visibly relaxed, closed her eyes, took a deep breath, let it out.

When she opened her eyes again, she smiled.

"Good."

"Good?"

She threw her blanket off, then tackled me, knocking me backward down the length of the couch.

"Yes, good. If you had said anything else, I would have got up and left and told the others that we were going to have to look for someone else."

Then she kissed me, and wrapped herself around me. I felt her pubic hair on my stomach, her breasts on my chest, and her fingers in my hair.

"I haven't said I'm staying," I said after she broke off the kiss.

"I know," she said. "But whether you stay in the band or not, you're staying with me."

Then she kissed me again.

I didn't know what to do but accept whatever she wanted to give me for the moment, and figure the rest out later.

TWENTY-FOUR

We arrived at the club to knowing smiles from Elise and Carol. Adelle seemed a little distant, but she smiled at Rose and greeted her with a hug.

What they were all thinking was, of course, all based on assumptions, even if they were true. We didn't tell them anything other than the story we told Mike. We went to have a talk, it got late, she spent the night in my bed while I slept on the couch. End of story.

They didn't believe it for a second.

Mike was there, too, but he stayed at the bar, chatting with Ross, leaving us to our work.

We ran a quick sound check, which was easy since nothing had really changed from the night before, then retired to the dressing room to get ready.

Again, I chose to leave the room while they got dressed. This time, though, there wasn't any argument. Adelle asked if I was staying, and Rose answered for me.

"No," she said. "Not tonight."

"Does that mean..."

"It doesn't mean anything," Rose said. "He's still trying to make the right decision for him, and for us, and we both decided that it was better just to focus on the show tonight and let tomorrow be what it will be."

We hadn't discussed any such thing, but it seemed to go over well with the others, and it set something resonating within my own head.

When the door shut behind me, I didn't sit down to wait. I went in search of Mike.

I had to get him off my mind. I had to get the whole situation out of my head, and just focus on the show.

I found Mike at the bar, but Ross wasn't anywhere near him. Mike was sitting alone, nursing what looked like a cola, though I suspected it was mixed with whiskey.

That's one problem with being a recovering alcoholic in a band. You have to work in venues where they serve alcohol, and resisting it becomes extremely difficult at times.

I hadn't noticed the night before, because I never went even close to the bar, and there had been so much on my mind with everything that I hadn't had time to think about it.

But as I stepped up next to Mike, I thought I could smell the whiskey in his drink. I had to shove the instantaneous thought of how just one couldn't hurt back into the recesses of my mind. One would always hurt.

"Did you really spend all night just talking with Rose?" Mike asked.

This was the friend, Mike. The guy who I'd spilled every dirty secret to for years. The guy who wanted to pal around.

"Yes," I lied. It was none of his business. If I stuck around in the band, it might get tricky, but for now, it wasn't important.

"Why don't I believe you?"

"Because you want me to have attached myself to her," I said. "You want me to stay with them after the show so that you can make a shitload of money off me, again."

"Hey," he said. "While that may be true, I'm still your friend. I'm trying to help you."

My anger was rising already, and I'd only spent two minutes with him, and hadn't even gotten around to what I wanted to talk about with him.

I shut it down.

The point was to eliminate the distraction, to focus on the show, not to get in an argument with him.

"I know you are," I said, "but your help is actually making things worse, right now."

"How? They drew a large crowd last night, and they're going to do it again. They'll make money off this couple of shows, and you will too. In fact," he said, reaching into his pocket. He pulled out a slip of paper and handed it to me. "Here's your check. You can now pay your rent for a couple months."

"Thanks," I said.

It was a check, made out to me for three thousand dollars, like we had agreed upon.

"You're welcome. If you don't want to stay in the band, I understand," he said. "But I think they're perfect for you. I think you're perfect for them."

"Like I was perfect for Savage Anarchy?"

"It worked for awhile," he said.

"Hardly," I said.

"But it..."

"No, no," I said, shutting my eyes. "I didn't come over here to argue about the past. I'm trying to get the current situation cleared up so I can go out there on the stage and have a good time."

"Okay. Look. If you really don't want to stay with these girls, I understand. But we need to find you another group. We need to get you back writing again."

Writing again. I couldn't remember the last time I wrote a song. I wrote a few early on with Savage Anarchy, but Johnny B. never accepted any of them, and I gave up trying. I tried to write a few for myself after that, but they never went anywhere, and with all the touring and the bullshit, I never had time to really put any effort into my own work.

And by the end of Savage Anarchy, I had no desire to write anything.

But Mike was right, even though I didn't want to hear it from him. I *did* need to write again. I needed to make songs, perform them.

The way Rose had changed from wanting to run me out of the room when we first met to wanting me to stay showed that I still had some ability. And the music was magic.

But this time, this time around, I was going to make my own choices.

"Look, Mike. I don't want to be an asshole about this," I said, starting out slowly. I really didn't want to get into another argument with him. "I know you're right. I do need to do those things, but this time, I think I need to make the choices on my own. I need to find the band on my own. I need to have control over what's happening, and I don't think I can do that with you as my manager."

Shit.

I hadn't actually intended to go that far. It was a break-up line, if there ever was one. I had just wanted to say I needed some time to figure this shit out.

But it was too late.

The skin on Mike's forehead tightened, his eyes narrowed, but he was looking up at me.

"What do you mean? We've always worked well together."

I heard hurt in his voice. His hand gripped his drink, but he sat still on his stool in his leather coat.

"Yes, we've made a lot of money together, but it's ruined me," I said. "Look what I've become. I've spent the last year, more, with a girlfriend who only wanted me for parties. I didn't do *anything* except hang out and spend money on other people. I don't want to be that way, anymore."

"You don't have to be. Join the girls, make music. I'll get us the money. It'll be good."

"But Mike, don't you see? They want to make it on their own. At least, Rose does. They want to learn how to be relevant on their own. They don't want to be Trent Richards and his Girls."

Mike took a sip of his drink.

"Alright. You've made your point. I won't force you to join the girls. I won't say another word about it. But you've got to decide soon what you're going to do. I need..."

Mike cut himself off, and put his drink to his lips again, and finished the glass.

"What were you going to say?" I asked. What did he need?

"Nothing," he said. "Just go out and play well tonight. Think about joining the girls. I think you're all perfect together, but if that's really not what you want to do, then we'll work out something else. Perhaps a solo career.

Perhaps we'll hold some tryouts, put another band together for you."

I sighed.

"Fine. Can you do something for me tonight?"

"Sure, what?"

"Don't come into the dressing room after the show. Don't push me to do anything right now. I want to enjoy the show, and I don't want to think about the future tonight. Whatever happens, I think this is the last time I'm going to play Narcoleptic Souls songs, and I want to remember it without any other drama surrounding it." I was thinking out loud as I said it, but it was true. I had no plans to play Narc Souls songs after tonight. If I stayed with the girls, or if I moved on, this was the last time. From now on, everything I did would be new.

"Fine," he said. "But I'll call you tomorrow."

"Okay."

"And you'll tell me what your plans are?"

"Sure."

He stood up, then gave me a hug. He hadn't done that in years.

We both knew something had changed. I don't think either of us could quite put a finger on what.

Maybe we were really breaking up, slowly.

And if we did, could I stand on my own? Could I manage my own career?

"Have a good show," he said, and patted me on the back.

"I'll do my best."

TWENTY-FIVE

I entered the dressing room again, and immediately, Rose presented me with the set list.

"What do you think?" she asked.

I looked through it.

Every one of their own songs was missing. Every song left on the list was a Narc Souls song.

"Your songs are missing. Are you sure you want to do that?"

She pulled the paper away from me, and I got a good look at everyone in the room for the first time. They wore their makeup like before, but every one of them was dressed in black. If they had any leg showing, it was covered in black stockings. They'd gone full on Narc Souls.

"We talked about it while you were out. What you said to me last night made a lot of sense. We're making some money doing this gig, which is good, but it's keeping us from moving toward the real goal."

"Wait. What did I say?"

"You said we've got to make the time to write songs."

"I don't understand how that changed the set list?

Elise stepped away from the mirror, where she had been adjusting her hair.

"We decided that tonight was our last Narc Souls show," she said.

The revelation stunned me. I didn't need to sit down, but it did take a moment to process.

"But I didn't say you had to quit playing Narc Souls songs."

"You didn't, but it makes the most sense," Rose said. "The only time we have to write songs together is during our rehearsal time. Currently, we use that for practicing for gigs mimicking some other band. Mike's methods for getting you in with us sucked ass, and we're all kind of pissed at him for that, but he saw the problem. He decided to fix it by injecting someone who could write better songs into the band, instead of telling us to take time off and just write songs."

"He likes the money," I said.

"He does," Rose said, "but this is about our future. We want you in the band, but we don't want it to be Trent and the Magnificent Chicks. We want to be a team. We want to be recognized as a group. And either way, if you join us or not, the only way to do that is to stop pretending to be someone else."

"All in."

"Yes," Carol said.

"So you're going to do one last blowout show as Narc Souls, and only Narc Souls."

"Yeah," Adelle said, grinning.

"And after tonight?"

"We dump all the songs and start over," Rose said. "We're going to write a hundred songs, pick the best dozen or so, and play those."

"That sounds fantastic," I said. It really did. Sitting around, writing, playing, picking the best of the songs instead of just going with the ones you can write in the limited time available while on tour.

"So you'll join us?" Rose asked.

I could hear the hope in her voice, and it did sound tempting. I liked them all, and when we played great songs, the effect was something I'd never felt before.

Did I really want to start from scratch?

The thought broke through me like an earthquake. That I even had the thought, considering the arguments I've had with Mike over the last couple days, astounded me.

I'd been arguing for starting from scratch, hadn't I?

Stop.

Just stop.

"I can't decide right now," I said. "Even if I wanted to make a decision right now, I told Mike I wasn't going to. I wanted tonight to be about the show, and only the show. And if you want to make tonight your last Narc Souls show, then I want to concentrate on making it the best damned Narc Souls show, ever."

"Right on," Carol said.

"Yeah," Rose said. "Better, even, than Narc Souls ever did on their own."

"Well, that's a given," I said.

"How's that?"

"I'm here," I said.

They all laughed, and I went to my closet to pull out my clothes.

Tonight would be Narcoleptic Souls, a chance to relive that time and do it right.

And so I shoved everything about the future into the back of my mind and shut the door on it.

I was going to do my very best to not fuck up the show with all that extra shit.

TWENTY-SIX

Just like the night before, the roar of the crowd intensified when I walked on stage. They knew who I was.

But this time, it was different for me. I climbed on stage for myself, for them. I climbed on stage, fully aware of the moment. I didn't even look for Mike. I didn't look for anyone. The only things that mattered were the people who climbed on stage with me, and the crowd.

And in that moment, I knew that the show we would perform for them would mark a turning point in my career. It wouldn't be one that anyone could see, but I would see it. I could feel it even then, before we played a note.

Right there, on that stage, the life I had led before would end. No more Narc Souls. No more Savage Anarchy and Johnny B. No more moping around my apartment wishing it all could have been different.

Rose and the others were on stage with me, and they chose to mark this night as a turning point for themselves. They would no longer pretend to be someone else.

I stared across the stage at Rose, and caught her staring right back at me, even through the makeup that hid her eyes. We shared the moment, even without speaking.

Neither of us knew what the future held.

But I knew, right there, that it wouldn't be an echo of the past.

Adelle cracked her sticks together, four violent motions that gave us the beat.

Rose and I continued to watch each other, even as we prepared our fingers to work the strings of our instruments.

The first note crashed through the crowd like a freight train, and chills ran up my spine.

I had lied to them when I said I couldn't make a decision. I had already made a decision.

I chose to live my life on my own terms, and if Mike's plans or Rose's plans, or anyone's plans, didn't fit with the things that I needed to be true to myself, I wouldn't give in and follow. That had only ever turned into disaster for me.

I would walk my path. I would write more songs. I would play music. I would do it all in the moment.

And for now, those moments would make me the only male member of an all female band.

The crowd roared.

ABOUT THE AUTHOR

Mark Fassett lives in western Washington with his wife, children, and cats. He's a fantasy and science fiction author whose novels include *Shattered*, *Minders*, and *Questioner's Shadow*. He's also written several novellas in those same genres. In the past, he had extensive experience in the mobile game business and was involved with some of the top selling titles at the time of their release, including multiple *Duke Nukem Mobile* games and *Guitar Hero World Tour Mobile*.

LEARN ABOUT NEW RELEASES

Visit http://markfassett.com/newsletter to join my mailing list and get notified about my newest releases!

FIND ME ONLINE

Blog — http://www.markfassett.com
Twitter — http://twitter.com/mark_fassett
Facebook — http://www.facebook.com/markfassett.writer
E-Mail — mark@markfassett.com